GUARDING KATELYN

A PARANORMAL SECURITY SERVICE NOVEL

J THOMPSON

To my Chapter Chicks.
You are all amazing
Thank you

CHAPTER ONE

Katelyn checked the lock on her front door for the fourth time. She pushed and pulled at the doorknob, testing it, checking it was definitely locked. After sliding across the chain, she sighed and finally let herself relax. All the windows were locked—she had double checked them as soon as she got home and again before checking the front door.

Safe... Rest, her bird chirped in her mind. Some would say she had issues. She would say it was her bird who had the issues.

Katelyn sighed and ignored the voice in her head. She was now of the mind that she couldn't be too careful, even if she lived two floors up in an apartment that had only two entry points. Safety was the most important thing for her, always had been. She'd just never taken it seriously before, hadn't believed the stories her parents had told her were true. Life had now got to the point that she carried pepper spray everywhere she went and a flip knife in her purse.

Katelyn turned the light off in the small bath-room—after checking it was empty—before walking into the main room of her home. The kitchen, living room and bedroom occupied the same space, but she had separated them using some of those fancy vintage screens. Their silk was worn with age, but she had fallen in love with them the moment she saw them at the market.

The apartment itself was tiny, but she was happy with it. It was pricey, but so were most places in London. Hell, she was lucky she was able to rent on her own. A lot of the other available places had been shared accommodation, giving her only a bedroom to herself. Although she was limited on space, she had finally found contentment.

Collecting her evening meal from where it had been heating in the microwave, she grabbed a fork before curling up on her bed. She relaxed against the pillows as she ate. She had turned all the lights off, her vision comfortably adjusting to the dim shine of the streetlight filtering through the window. Its golden glow gilded the room, and as Katelyn ate, she settled further into the pillows. Outside, the hustle and bustle of London could still be heard; cars with their beeping horns, the laughter of the many enjoying their nightly ventures. The sounds had become Katelyn's lullaby, sounds she was now completely used to and would miss if they weren't present.

This had become her routine now. She spent her days doing the job she loved, photographing everything from people to buildings, and her evenings tucked up safe in her small home, watching the world go by.

The food quickly gone, she placed the container on her bedside table before picking up her large mug of hot chocolate. Wrapping her hands around the porcelain, she blew away the steam.

Life six months ago had been much different. She had been convinced there was no way out. Only, she had proved stronger than she thought. A shiver travelled up her spine as she thought of what could have been, and for the second time this day, her bird chirped.

Shhh, we escaped... We free.

Katelyn sighed and shifted on the bed. Her bird hated being reminded of what had happened. She hated the fact she wasn't allowed out as much, but she had little choice.

Katelyn wasn't just a normal girl, finding her way in the big city. No, she was one of a few breeds of shifter, of paranormal. Paranormals had, as an entirety, come out in the UK not long after they had in the USA, and as such, they were, in a way, famous. But not her. Katelyn kept her animal side quiet, shifting only when her bird was desperate for an escape. It was all well and good being able to shift, especially if you were a wolf, panther or even a dragon, but it wasn't as simple when you were a bird of myth and legend. As a phoenix, she was rare, and most of the stories that told of how her kind had magical properties, were all, in fact, true. True to the point her breed of shifter was now hunted.

Katelyn had always embraced being a phoenix, but that didn't mean she had revelled in it. At times, Katelyn had felt lacking as a paranormal in comparison to others. Other beings could breathe fire, grow claws and teeth that had the ability to rip someone's face off. There were even some that had the gift of being able to vanish, a gift Katelyn, on more than one occasion, had wished for.

A phoenix, though... Well, Katelyn's bird, the other half of her soul, couldn't do any of that. In fact, she was the complete opposite of being fierce —not that Katelyn blamed her. They both lacked greatly in the defensive skill department—other than a set of three inch claws which would no doubt break on contact. Katelyn was lucky to be where she was at that very moment.

Katelyn and her bird sighed at the same time. Their skills centred around the subtle art of healing, and for a paranormal, that was a very important task indeed. Where most were immortal, some wounds could, in fact, cause a premature death. In the past, when wars were waged, there was always a phoenix behind the scenes, patching up warriors and sending them back into the fray. It was a proud position, and her kind were greatly sought. Now, her kind were pursued for a different reason.

Ever since she was a child, her parents had told her not to show her bird off, no matter how stunning she was to behold. The legends only hinted of the magnificence. They couldn't compare to seeing one in person, with their colours varying from golds all the way through to purples and everything in between. The tail feathers were long and elegant, sweeping down at over a metre in length, making her bird appear bigger than she actually was. It was those tail feathers that held another gift, one few knew about. They were capable of absorbing energy, mainly lighting. The uses were unclear to Katelyn. Her parents had never divulged that bit of information, and if truth be told, it had been lost to the history books too.

Her parents had also encouraged Katelyn to avoid making friends, to avoid all contact. But as she grew older, she began to understand how lonely she became. She craved contact, craved being with people, and if it meant she had to suppress her bird, then she would, because the idea of being alone her whole life, hurt.

As a photographer, Katelyn dealt with people every day, and she loved it, loved interacting. She had been warned that people would stop at nothing to profit from what a phoenix could do. Their feathers, tears and blood all had magical properties. A phoenix on the black market was a goldmine. Alive, they could fund small operations for years. Dead, they could be sold for instant cash. As a young chick, she had never really taken the warnings seriously, thinking her parents had made them up to scare her.

Unfortunately, everything they had warned her about was true.

She had been happy living just outside of Manchester, in the small town of Salford. As with all Phoenix families, her parents encouraged her to move into her own place. They did this so they wouldn't be clustered together. Being clustered like that made them an even bigger target for those who dealt in the black market and profited from shifter trafficking.

So they separated for their own protection, and Katelyn felt the sting of loneliness regularly. She missed her mum and dad, missed her younger sister. They spoke daily, either by phone call from a local phone box or over a special website that had been created for her kind. It was a chat room of sorts, keeping her kind from all around the world up to date on information about places they should avoid, known dealers, and safe havens. Ashes.com had been her companion since her escape from the north. Chatting to other phoenixes had helped to hold back that sting of being alone, but not for long.

A yawn fought its way to the surface, and Katelyn placed her mug on the table before sliding under the covers. She smiled to herself as she thought of the exciting day she had coming up; a chance to photograph the Fabergé collection for a magazine.

Slowly, she drifted off, her earlier worries forgotten as she dreamed of diamonds and pearls bathed in red flames.

CHAPTER TWO

T rent shifted once again in his seat. Even in business class he struggled to get comfortable. His size just didn't allow it, and Hilda had refused his request for one of those swanky first-class seats. At well over six feet and wider than Dwayne Johnson, Trent had little choice but to put up and shut up. Hilda was not only his friend but his boss as well, the driving force behind the Paranormal Security Service. It had been created to help protect paranormals, and not just from humans, but from other races as well. Trent's main role had been protection detail. With his size and strength, he was usually the first choice. Not that he minded. It was something to keep his mind occupied.

The air hostess had helped alleviate his discomfort, making sure he was comfortable for the majority of the flight. Hell, she had made it obvious that if he gave her the nod, she would drop her panties and give up the goods.

He had been tempted... but decided against it. She was a stunning little thing, he would admit, but she did nothing for him. It had been this way for a while, ever since he hit the youthful age of one hundred. His brain was on board, but his body was simply not interested in the opposite sex, be it human or paranormal, and it pissed him off. He loved sex, and from the reactions of the few partners he had bedded, he wasn't half bad at it.

Trent chewed on his thumb as he looked out the window, watching the fields and trees growing ever closer as the plane circled and descended towards the landing strip.

A new life in London awaited him. He was ready for it. He cared deeply for his friends back in the US but had become increasingly detached as, one by one, they fell to Cupid's bow, each finding a mate that settled and grounded them, until he was left on his own with no clue what the hell his body, mind or heart wanted. He felt torn, at a loss, and hoped the change in scenery, as well as helping

Suzanna set up the new office of the Paranormal Security Service, would help.

The beep of the tanoy caused Trent to look up, although there was nothing to look up at.

Good morning, this is your captain speaking. On behalf of myself and my co-pilot, we would like to thank you for flying with BAS Airways. The time in London is 9:28a.m. And the weather is cloudy, sitting at a cool twelve degrees centigrade. We hope you have had a pleasant flight and will fly with us again.

Please, on landing, make sure you have all your belongings.

We wish you a pleasant day.

Cloudy... Ha! Trent smirked. London was famous for having dull weather, or perhaps that was England in general. He had always wanted to travel, but had more exotic climes than London in mind.

His stomach flipped as the plane started to descend faster, readying itself for touchdown. His senses picked up on the landing wheels lowering, and he heard heartbeats all over the plane speed up in response.

Ten minutes later, they touched down. Any longer and Trent would have started to get twitchy.

He had been sat far too long, and both sides of his nature wanted out of the metal tube. He wanted away from the constant flirtatious looks being sent his way from not only the females, but some of the males as well. As a paranormal, he was lucky to have not aged since the day he turned thirty, but also thanks to his other side, the one that wasn't a gargoyle, he gave off an aura to attract those of the opposite sex. He spent most of his life ignoring that part. He didn't want nor need it. But sometimes, like now, it slipped around his defences and attracted attention he did not want. Not that he knew what it was. It was something his mother had never felt the need to tell him. All she had whispered upon occasion, when she was drunk, was demon. That had never narrowed it down as there were many factions of demons that resided around the world.

Sliding out of the plush leather, Trent collected his duffle bag from the overhead compartment and made his way to the exit. That's all the luggage he had. Clothes, he could buy anywhere, and he had ever set down enough roots in one place to acquire things. If he was honest, as long as there was a bed, food and a bathroom, he was set.

Moving quickly past his fellow passengers, he

growled under his breath, annoyed with how slow they were. Trent's extended period in such a confined space made him twitchy. He needed out. Now.

"So, how was your flight?" Suzanna's posh English accent pulled Trent from his thoughts as he looked out the window of the limo he had been collected in. His new co-boss had been waiting for him at arrivals. She was stunning, and had gained looks of admiration from every single person in that airport. Men drooled and women looked on with envy.

Yet Trent felt nothing. It was like he had turned to stone inside.

Suzanna was tall, over six feet, and had long platinum blonde hair that had been braided and fell to her arse. Her body was slender. There was something almost predatory about her, but he knew she wasn't a vampire. He had not been told what kind of paranormal she was, and it would be rude of him to ask.

"As flights go, it was ok," he answered, and smiled, a small lift of his lips. "Glad to be back on the ground though."

"Yeah, I feel the same way after a flight. Somehow, being trapped in a long metal tube hurtling at high speed doesn't make me feel all that safe." She chuckled before changing the subject. "I've set you up in a flat in the same building as the office, just until you get your bearings. London is a rabbit warren. Even after my long stay, I still get lost."

"Thank you. I really appreciate it. How many have we got on the books?" Trent asked, wanting to get on with the work he had been assigned.

"At the moment, five, including yourself. A couple of shifters, a demon, and a fairy." He watched as she counted them off on her fingers. "The shifters are good workers, have put a lot of effort in. The demon and fairy, though... You may need to help me with. They seem to not like each other. All of them are on protection detail, which I know you have experience with. So they are your babies." Suzanna shrugged.

"I will see what I can do, and I would appreciate any work you can send my way. I like to keep busy," Trent admitted.

"You don't want to settle in?" she asked, and he could see the curiosity in her eyes. She wanted to know more. She could want all she liked.

"No need," was all he said as the limo pulled in

front of a large building. A small golden plaque was screwed to the outside. The only evidence of what was housed inside.

PSS - London Branch.

"I like your style. Go straight in and up to the top floor, and I will see you in the office shortly," Suzanna called as she slid out of the limo after him and made her way to the glass doors.

"Coffee will be waiting."

CHAPTER THREE

T he apartment—or flat, as the Brits like to say —was surprisingly spacious and a hell of a lot bigger than he had expected. Hell, even the bathroom was bigger than his bedroom back home, Trent thought as he poked his head into the room. Its door was the first on the right in the hallway. To the left were another three doors. All were closed.

Technically, his place in the US hadn't been his home. Trent hadn't truly felt at home since he had been a child. He'd had places to stay and sleep, but nowhere he could put down roots.

Bag in hand, Trent walked through the hallway and out into the open-plan living area. The apartment was fully furnished and had been decorated in a simple, contemporary style. No garish colours assaulted his senses, only subtle greys, black and white

Dumping his bag on the sofa, Trent stood and looked out the window that travelled the full length of the kitchen and living area. His new view was a strange contrast to what he was used to. The traffic was the same in any city, no matter where in the world you travelled, yet the buildings here were not as high, and, surprisingly, there was a lot more greenery than back home.

Home... Where was home for a loner such as him? He didn't think he had ever felt like he belonged anywhere.

Stretching his bulky arms above his head, Trent watched the flow of traffic below, watched as cars flew by on the wrong side of the road and wondered if moving halfway across the world would settle him and his inner demons or just placate them for a time. That was something he would deal with if and when it happened. His darker side had always struggled to settle anywhere.

The sooner he started work, the better. Yes, the service was brand new, almost unknown, but from his experience across the pond, it would not take long for the clients to come flooding in. He just hoped Suzanna knew that and had plenty of bums on seats to deal with the workload that was sure to come. Trent didn't at all mind taking on his fair share—hell, he encouraged it—but he wasn't about to spend twenty-four hours a day, seven days a week, working. He ideally wanted to see something of this city, and maybe find that distraction he craved so much.

Turning away from the view, Trent collected his bag and made his way into what would now be his bedroom. He would explore behind the other two doors later, but for now it could wait. From his bag, he pulled out some clothes and toiletries, then went to have a shower. He would freshen up and then head down to the office. It was still early, so surely, he could find something to do. After all, Suzanna did promise coffee.

CHAPTER FOUR

C*lick, click, click, click...*
The sound of the shutter on Katelyn's camera repeated as she fired shots off rapidly. Its music made her heart feel light as she did the job she adored. She grinned when she stood up, her thumb quickly scrolling through the pictures as she assessed her most recent images. Picture after picture of the same scene turned her grin into a frown. Every picture was great, only she wasn't happy with any of them. Something seemed off with each one. The lighting didn't hit right, and when it did, the subject had moved.

Grumbling under her breath, Katelyn pulled the camera back up, ready to snap a few more shots. She had been contracted to take pictures of the local wildlife, and wildlife was what her employers were going to get, even if this swan strutting its stuff in front of her wasn't being the most compliant model.

Click, click, click...

"That's it, superstar, I'm done with you," Katelyn called to the swan, who, deciding she was no longer worth its time or attention, spread its spectacular wings and jumped from the bank, back into the murky waters of the Thames.

He was a braver soul than her. Katelyn had heard stories of what lurked in the most famous river in the UK, and it wasn't monsters. She shuddered at the thought as she placed the lens cover back on and hung her favourite toy around her neck.

Her day had been well spent; a morning of editing pictures for a local gallery, a spot of lunch by the river, and then tackling her wildlife assignment. Now all she had to do was navigate the London traffic and get home before dark.

She hadn't always been afraid of the dark, but now she hated the shadows that lurked in every corner, every alley, and the feeling she was being watched never went away. But she had made sure to cover her tracks well. Plus, she wasn't of use to anyone. No one would bother searching for her.

That was what Katelyn kept telling herself, even though it was probably a lie—a huge one at that. She would broach the subject on Ashes, though she didn't expect an answer; a lot of her fellow firebirds clammed up tighter than a banker's wallet when it came time to discuss the proverbial axe above their heads. Ashes.com did serve its purpose though; it managed to do safely what couldn't usually be done. To bring together phoenix shifters from around the world without the risk of them being in the same room. It meant she could chat to others like her and find out what they knew. It also meant they could share information on the situation with the black market hunters.

The chat room had been live for only two months, but Katelyn had been one of the first to sign up. She had been eager—no, desperate for any sort of company, even if it was only over the internet. Nobody knew how lonely she actually was, and how much she missed her family. To be a being of legend shouldn't mean she should be alone —dammit, she wasn't a ring bearer. Katelyn chuckled at her own nerdy joke, who the hell didn't love *Lord of the Rings*. Her chuckles became a grunt as she picked her way up the grass verge and back onto the path.

Once on solid ground, she took a few more snaps of the river as it lazily flowed, capturing the silhouette of Big Ben in the background before she finally put her camera away. She kept moving forward, one foot in front of the other.

"Hey, watch it," a deep voice called out as large hands gripped her shoulders to steady her. She had ploughed straight into the chest of a man on his own walk.

"Oh my gosh, I'm so, so sorry."

Katelyn looked up, and up, into a classically handsome face, only to freeze when her gaze connected with his eyes. Green—bright green— flashed, giving her the briefest glimpse into something she recognized as evil that was hidden within. She recalled his face in the deepest recesses of her memory but couldn't remember his name. She didn't want to.

This was what she had been running from.

The urge to scream and run away hit Katelyn hard, but she knew if she succumbed, she would be openly admitting what she was. Only phoenix's ran. She refused. Instead, she faked a smile and laughed as she stepped out of his reach, his hand falling to his side. She kept up the pretence that she didn't know who he was.

"I really am sorry. I should look where I am going."

"It's fine, sweetheart. I don't mind being manhandled, especially if the culprit looks like you." His charming voice did nothing but put her nerves on edge, sending shivers down her spine and making her stomach churn. This was how they caught you: charm. But Katelyn had learned her lesson, and she would never make the same mistake twice.

"Charmer," she laughed again. "Sorry again, I've got to shoot." She smiled and gestured to her bag before she walked off. Katelyn sped up and moved to join a group of walkers, slotting into the crowd until she was able to get to the street. If she had any luck, she'd find a black cab to take her home.

Katelyn felt like she held her breath the entire time it took her to grab a taxi and get home. She continuously looked behind her, expecting to see not only the man from the park, but also her ex.

Six months earlier, Katelyn had been in what she thought was love. She had fallen head over heels for a six-feet-four, dirty blonde, blue-eyed angel, who had charmed her, wooed her, and bedded her. For Katelyn, he had been it. He had been perfect, had been her main focus.

Their relationship was too perfect to be true, until after a few months, he started to snap at her for no reason. He didn't like her going out on her own, which she was used to, but he had started to tell her she couldn't go out at all. Even when she needed to do her job. Duncan, her knight, her first love, was not who she had thought he was. His odd behaviour culminated in Katelyn being locked away. She learned then that everything she had been told was a complete lie.

Duncan had sought her out for one reason and one reason only: she was a mark, a target, because she was a phoenix. He had never wanted her heart, nor did he care about her. She had figured that much when he backhanded across the room after she argued with him, demanding that she be allowed to leave the house. He had looked her in the eye and told her she was nothing more than a profit making machine. He would use her, use her hair, her blood, and her tears, until there was nothing left. And even in death, her body would make him profit.

Katelyn had felt like he ripped her heart out. She felt betrayed and used, for unlike her family, she had refused to cower and hide in the shadows.

Instead, she had waited for him to leave, knowing he would be out with his fellow demons hunting some unsuspecting soul. He may have locked her in the house, but she was not as weak as he had assumed. Katelyn had packed her bags —what little she had—broken the lock on the back door and fled into the night. That night, all she knew was that she needed to get away. Far away.

As Katelyn locked the door to her apartment, checked and double checked it, a part of her mind was convinced she was being silly. That the man she had seen was simply that, just a man. Only, she could never forget the eyes; the eyes of the being that enjoyed inflicting pain on others. Duncan and his friends were demons; paranormals of the lowest kind, who preyed on the weak for their own gain. These were the monsters Katelyn had been warned about as a child, and now they had found her.

She needed help, because there was no way

she could run forever. But she didn't know who to trust. She didn't know where to turn.

Moving to the bed, Katelyn picked up her laptop. Quickly turning it on, she headed straight for Ashes.com. Her words felt rushed as she typed them, her fingers flowing over the keyboard.

Fawkes17: *SOS. Need help. I think they found me. Can you assist?*

Hotstuff_28 has entered the chat room.

Hotstuff_28: *Who's found you? Where are you?*

Fawkes17: *The hunters. London. I'm in London, but I don't know if I can stay here.*

Hotstuff_28: *London? I may know of someone. Have you ever heard of the PSS?*

Fawkes17: *No, I haven't. Can they really help?*

Hotstuff_28: *If anyone can, they can. They've just opened an office in London.*

Fawkes17: *Thank you... I don't know what else to do.*

Hotstuff_28: *Don't give up hope. Hope is all we have left. Right, I've got to go. I hope that helped. Please keep me posted. Let me know you are ok?*

Hotstuff_28 has left the chat room.

Katelyn's heart was racing. She wanted to grab her bags and race out the door, leaving London and the hunters behind. But that would mean starting a new life again. She hated the idea. She hated running, but what was the alternative?

Stay, with the risk of being caged for being a phoenix, or a run for the rest of her life, never settling, never belonging.

Bringing up the search engine on her laptop, Katelyn typed in the company that could possibly be the key to her survival.

PSS-London.

Katelyn tossed and turned all night, her body too wired to allow sleep, her mind, instead, taking her back to the day she made a terrible mistake.

She had met Duncan while out taking pictures of a sunrise. His appearance seemed coincidental at the time, only now she knew better.

He had been charming, made her feel special,

and gained her trust quickly. She had given every-thing to him, though never came clean about what kind of shifter she was. He had never pushed to know, which, at the time, put her at ease, but now she knew he had already figured it out, and it was the only reason he was with her.

A sob forced its way up her throat as Katelyn moved onto her back and stared up at the ceiling of her flat. She remembered the day everything had gone south for her. She recalled it like it had only just happened, the same fear now ripping through her.

Katelyn wandered through the small two-bedroomed house she shared with Duncan and made sure everything was in its place. She had blitzed the house, cleaning everywhere and every-thing as soon as he had messaged her to say he had a surprise for her. He liked doing that, bringing home small gifts for her. Duncan made her feel special just for being her, not a phoenix.

Maybe she would finally tell him what she was. She trusted him.

"Katy," Duncan called from the front door, his nickname for her making her tummy jump with butterflies.

"I'm here." She quickly made her way through

to meet him, smiling when she saw he had a large bouquet of flowers in his hand. He did this every day, even when the house was already full of blooms.

"Oh, they are beautiful." Katelyn smiled and took them, instantly going in to smell the selection of roses and lilies. Distracted, Katelyn missed the other male that had entered the room. It was only when she looked up that she saw the usual, relaxed demeanour of her boyfriend had changed. Instead, he looked, in short, evil. Katelyn's heart faltered. Her bird, for the first time since she had started seeing Duncan, rose up, chirping in her head about danger.

"Everything ok, Duncan?" she asked, unable to keep the nervousness out of her voice.

"Oh yes, everything is perfect," he drawled as he approached, forcing Katelyn to back up until she hit the worktop that signalled the entrance to the kitchen. Katelyn held her breath as he lifted his hand to stroke her cheek, his eyes going from the blue she loved to a deep scarlet. His face began to change, giving her a glimpse into what he really was.

"Oh, my dear, you have given me so much, but there is more to take... You do know how valuable you are, don't you?" he asked, but continued, not waiting for an answer. "Everything about you is worth something, my sweet, sweet bird." His breath washed across her face, a putrid smell that made her gag and realise what all the flowers had been for.

The male she thought would be her mate was, in fact, a demon, one that needed the constant smell of flowers to assist with hiding his true nature.

"You're a demon," Katelyn gasped, and she realised what a fool she had been, trusting in the first handsome face that had come along. Her parents had been right. No one could be trusted, and now she had paid the price.

"Oh yes." He grinned, and she ripped her face away from his touch and pushed at his chest, desperate to get him away from her.

His features changed, morphing into a hideous creature. Katelyn gasped as he made to grab her again, but this time, Katelyn reacted, swiping out with her hand in an effort to get away.

"You fucking bitch," Duncan's guttural voice screeched out. Katelyn had little time to react as a clawed hand swept in front of her vision, the force of the impact sending her to the floor where her head connected with the kitchen counter.

Struggling to remain conscious, Katelyn was

dragged into darkness, and all the while her bird screamed in fear.

That had been the start of her week from hell, one long week before she had managed to escape. A week of regretting all her decisions since she had left the safety of her parents' home. Regrets of a life she had dreamed of but could never have.

A life she would now spend on the run, especially if the PSS couldn't help her.

CHAPTER FIVE

T rent tapped the down arrow on his keyboard more than a little enthusiastically. To be honest, if he hit it any harder his finger would go through the plastic key. The sound seemed to really annoy the young nymph on the front desk. That had to be the reason why she kept shooting him glares from behind her own computer screen.

Due to the fact the office was brand new, work was slow. Trent had already gone through the files for the guys who had been placed on the books. Three werewolves, Scott, Mike and Ben, had been the first to sign up, and they showed promise. Trent wasn't sure if they were brothers, but they all looked very similar. Although, werewolves all tended to look the same. All were keen to be busy, a lot like himself, but there was a wildness in their eyes that put Trent on edge. He would monitor them, but as long as they worked hard, he wouldn't say anything.

The only other to sign up as a guard was a male called Conrad. He had a file, yet it revealed nothing but his name and current address, along with his skills. Trent hoped to meet with him soon, just so they knew who he was. The last thing he needed was Suzanna thinking he was trying to boss them around or step on her toes.

The only thing he really, really wanted to know was what kind of paranormal Suzanna was. He felt like it was on the edge of his tongue, but every time he tried to sit and think, his mind went completely blank. Her own file said nothing, which didn't surprise him. What did was the in-depth knowledge that was written in his own. She must have received it from Hilda, but even he wasn't aware his old boss knew so much about him. His past wasn't something he liked to discuss with anyone—hell, he didn't even like thinking about it. It was in the past, and as far as Trent was concerned, it would remain there, buried deep.

Closing the window he was looking through,

Trent turned his attention to the current diary, making sure all jobs were covered. Suzanne had basically made him a sort of operations manager, so he was in charge of making sure the jobs were completed and done to a high standard.

Only two of the werewolves were currently employed, being used as bouncers at a local night-club that catered for paranormals. They had been having issues with vandalism and continuous break-ins. So, if anyone could sniff out the culprits, it would be Scott and Ben.

Voices filtered through to his office from the front desk, one of which was the high-pitched voice of Margi. The sound made his left eye twitch as it seemed to get higher and higher.

"Does she actually take a breath?" Trent muttered under his breath, trying to zone out, yet the voices seemed determined to be heard.

"You don't understand, ma'am. You cannot just walk in. You have to make an appointment."

"Please don't call me ma'am. I am not a ma'am. I bloody well tried to make an appointment. Multiple times. But guess what, your website wouldn't let me, and when I tried to call, my calls went straight to an answer phone."

"We are a busy company."

"Yeah, it certainly looks like it. You and your nail file are real busy. You know what, leave it. I don't want to deal with judgemental arses like you, anyway."

Trent perked up at the sound of the secondary voice. Its husky tone called his attention, but before he could get out of his chair to see who the owner was, she stormed out, leaving a flustered Margi behind.

"Who was that?" Trent asked as he walked out of his office.

"She didn't leave a name," Margi huffed and moved to pick up her nail file.

"So why was she unable to make an appointment? What's wrong with the phones and the website?" Trent asked, actually curious. If this had happened back in the US, Hilda would have stripped someone's hide already.

"Oh, errr..." The nymph stumbled over her words, unable to come up with an excuse.

Turning, Trent ignored her attempts to clear her own actions and moved towards the door. Pedestrians passed by, jostling to get past each other, only his attention caught on someone only a foot from the door. Bright red hair cascaded down her back. Her head was bowed, and he could see she had folded her arms around herself. She was tiny. If she stood against him, she would only reach his chest.

Perfect height...

That thought surprised him. Pushing through the glass door, Trent slowly approached. The female, whoever she was, emanated despair in waves.

"Excuse me?" Trent called out softly, not wanting to startle her, but also desperate for her to turn around. Her head whipped round, until finally she looked at him, and Trent could do little but suck in a breath.

She was stunning. The bright red hair framed a pale, heart-shaped face. Amber eyes stared back at him, filled with emotion and on the verge of releasing a torrent of tears. Small freckles covered her nose, which was dainty and pert, and her lips... both full, pink, and begging to be kissed.

His body reacted instantaneously, no longer stone. Instead, heat boiled from within. Images, erotic pictures, filled his head, making his heart pound in his chest, until he registered a single tear that had fallen from her right eye.

She still said nothing, only looked at him, waiting for him to continue.

"Are you ok?" he asked as he took a step forward. This female was different, so different in fact, that she drew him in, making that side of him that could never settle almost sigh in relief.

"No, not really, but I'm sure someone else has it worse." Her voice had a husky edge to it, like she had spent all night screaming or smoked twenty a day for the last few years.

"Is that why you wanted an appointment?" he asked, eager to know what she had wanted and if he could help. Not just the company but him personally. He had always felt he had a sense of duty to protect those smaller than him. The look of despair on her face just made that need greater. The need to make her smile.

"Why do you want to know?" she answered defensively. Moving her arms that had been wrapped around her stomach, she stood a little higher and folded them across her chest. He didn't blame her for getting defensive. He hadn't exactly given her any reason to trust him.

"Sorry. Let me introduce myself. My name's Trent, and I work for the PSS. I couldn't help over-hearing your discussion with the receptionist and thought I would try to help." Trent paused before he turned his big body and pulled the door open, waving a hand through. "Please, come back in and we can talk in my office." He smiled, and for the first time in his existence, he wished he wasn't as big as he was. His size intimidated most, and that was the last thing he wanted to do to this female.

Stepping forward, she returned his smile, only it didn't reach her eyes. Just as she passed him, she looked up at him. Trent was lost in those amber eyes of hers that sparkled with gold.

"Thank you. My name is Katelyn. It's nice to meet you, Trent."

CHAPTER SIX

Katelyn didn't think her heart had stopped hammering in her chest at all in the past three hours. She had planned to look up the PSS for some help, but she hadn't thought she would have to do it as soon as she woke up. She and her bird were usually out for the count when they slept, only this time her bird had woken her early, warning her.

Fear had taken over when she heard someone attempting the locks on her door. She had heard the voices and panicked. Katelyn dressed as quickly and quietly as she could, then grabbed her prepacked bag for emergencies and climbed out of the window and onto the fire escape. It was a risk she'd had to take, for all she knew, they could have been waiting outside for her. For this night, luck was on her side as she snuck down a side alley that brought her out onto the main road and into the throngs of people already making their way through London.

Katelyn had walked a good three miles in the direction of the office before hiding around the back of a small coffee shop. She hated this. Her short time of freedom had not been enough. Katelyn had finally found a sense of independence, had managed to not look over her shoulder every minute, and now her sense of safety had been ripped from her. Her parents had spoken only truth when they said to be a phoenix was to be caged. Not necessarily by hunters, but by their own mere existence.

Caged. Trapped for simply existing, for being herself... This was not the life Katelyn had dreamed of when she was a little girl. This was a living nightmare, one she had little chance of escaping. Her only hope now rested on whether anyone could help her at the Paranormal Security Service.

If not, well... Katelyn didn't dare think of what could happen if they couldn't. Leaving the coffee house, she had followed her phone's sat nav to the large, imposing building that housed the people who unknowingly held her hopes and future in the palm of their hand.

Without thinking and having the possibility of changing her mind, Katelyn pushed through the large glass door and into the quiet foyer. Everything was white, crisp and clean. There was a single large desk with four open doors behind. From the briefest of glimpses, Katelyn could see offices. But at that moment, she had to speak to the gorgeous blonde that sat behind the desk, filing her perfect nails.

Katelyn regretted her choice of outfit for the day—plain jeans and a thick hoodie—but it had been the first thing to hand. She had left her hair down, but it had been messed by the breeze and from trying to tackle her way through the streets of London. She felt grimy and totally out of her depth, but she stepped forward anyway.

"Err, excuse me?" she asked. The receptionist didn't look up, nor did she stop filing her nails.

"Have you got an appointment?"

"Err, no, sorry. Is this the office for the Paranormal Security Service?" she asked, and finally was graced with the full attention of the receptionist, who gently placed the nail file on the desk and looked at her. Katelyn wasn't used to seeing other unique species, and the lady in front of her was definitely not human. The way her bright blue eyes glowed gave her away.

"Yes, it is, but you need an appointment."

"Well, can I make one? It's kind of urgent," Katelyn answered, starting to get irritated by the way the receptionist was looking at her. The blonde gave an irritated sigh.

"There is a bit of a wait," the receptionist responded, not even looking at her computer screen.

Katelyn clenched her teeth until she was sure they would break, giving herself to the count of ten before she replied. "So, can no one see me today? It's kind of urgent."

"You don't understand, ma'am." The sneer in the blonde's voice made Katelyn twitch. "You cannot just walk in. You have to make an appointment."

Katelyn took one long, deep breath in before she answered. Once again, her hopes had been dashed. Did she really want to deal with a company that gave people like the receptionist a chance to belittle others, beings that needed help, not judgement? They got that enough from the humans.

"Please don't call me ma'am. I'm not a ma'am," Katelyn started, irritation now lacing her words. "I bloody well tried to make an appointment. Multiple times. But guess what, your website wouldn't let me, and when I tried to call, my calls went straight to an answer phone."

"We are a busy company," she replied, her eyes glowing brighter. Katelyn could feel her bird pushing, wanting to poke her eyes out.

"Yeah, it certainly looks like it. You and your nail file are real busy," Katelyn snapped. "You know what, leave it. I don't want to deal with judgemental arses like you, anyway."

Without waiting for a reply, Katelyn turned and headed for the door. Pushing once again against the glass, she let out a long breath as she moved out into the fresh air and onto the pavement. She didn't move completely from the doorway, not wanting to get trampled by the throngs of people. Instead, she wrapped her arms around her waist and bent her head.

The PSS had been her last hope. Yes, she could move again, try a different city, possibly a different country, but wouldn't that just lead to the same outcome? Spending the rest of her life running and looking over her shoulder all the time was not what she called the most perfect life. Even so, it was the lesser of two evils.

To be captured or to flee.

Those were her options, as pathetic as they were.

"Excuse me," a deep voice called from behind. The sound flowed over her irritated nerves, soothing them. Her bird, which had been ready to burst from her skin, shivered in response and almost purred. Phoenixes didn't purr—not that she was aware of anyway. Whipping her head around, her breath caught in her throat.

A huge male stood just behind her. He stood at well over six feet, and his build...wow. The only person she could compare him to was Dwayne 'The Rock' Johnson. But this male would dwarf even him. Muscles flexed and moved, even as he stood still. Dressed in a t-shirt and jeans, he was breath-taking, like something straight out of a romance novel.

Katelyn slowly turned her whole body to face his, not yet trusting herself to speak, afraid anything she tried to say would just come out as a squeak.

. . .

"Are you ok?" he asked as he took a step towards her. Usually, Katelyn would have stepped back in response, but this time she held firm. His voice was deep, and his accent was most certainly not English.

Katelyn shook her head a little, both answering his question and trying to rid her gutter-bound mind of all the delicious images of this male and the muscles he was carrying.

"No, not really, but I'm sure someone else has it worse." It was true. It could be worse. She could already be in the hands of the hunters. Katelyn shivered and watched the male's eyes narrowing slightly as he caught the movement.

"Is that why you wanted an appointment?" he asked and moved again until only a foot or so separated them. His question filtered through her hazy mind and brought both her bird and herself back to the present.

"Why do you want to know?" she answered defensively. Moving her arms that had been wrapped around her stomach, she stood a little higher and folded them across her chest. Who was this male and why did he want to know?

"Sorry. Let me introduce myself. My name's Trent, and I work for the PSS. I couldn't help overhearing your discussion with the receptionist and thought I would try to help." She watched as he smiled slightly and turned his big body, reaching out with long arms to open the glass door of the building. Katelyn's heart stopped for a second, before restarting as hope once again welled within her. He wanted to help. Could he, though?

"Please, come back in and we can talk in my office." He smiled again, and this time, the flutter of her heart and the butterflies in her stomach had nothing to do with hope. This reaction was purely lust-driven. He was gorgeous. It was that simple. And for some reason, her bird had taken a liking to him. The purring in her head now vibrated through her body.

"Stop it, dammit," she whispered, before stepping forward and returning his smile. It was the best she could do in this situation. When she looked up into his dark eyes, Katelyn felt shaky. Like her world, her world that had become nightmare, might just have changed. Whether it was for the better, she didn't know. She would take that chance.

"Thank you. My name is Katelyn. It's nice to

meet you, Trent." Her voice came out huskier than she wanted, and as she stepped back into the foyer, she felt the heat of him at her back. It felt... good.

"Margi," he called out from behind her, "bring some coffee to my office." His voice seemed harsh, until she realised he was talking to the receptionist who now was firing daggers in her direction.

"This way, Katelyn." The way he said her name almost made her knees weak.

"You're not English?" she asked as she followed him into a large office, which only had a desk and two chairs. She watched as he pulled out a chair for her, before he moved around to the other side of the desk. Slowly, she sat, waiting for his answer and to hear his voice. His accent did things to her body —not that she would admit that.

"No, I'm from the US. Just flew in to London yesterday." He smirked at her as he searched through his draws for something. "Still getting my bearings."

Bringing out a pad and a pen, he placed them on the desk before leaning back in his chair. The black t-shirt he wore stretched across his wide chest, and Katelyn could have sworn she heard the fabric strain under the force. Hell, a part of her—possibly her bird—encouraged it to rip so she could catch a glimpse of the solid flesh beneath.

Hussy, she thought. Her bird purred even louder.

"So, how can the PSS help you?"

Ok! This was what she was here for. But how did she do this without giving away what she was? She didn't want anyone to know. Telling others would put herself in more danger, and even if she was lucky enough to gain the friendship of people who really cared, she refused to put them at risk. She knew the type of people that hunted her, and they would stop at nothing.

A part of her didn't want to involve anyone for that reason, but she had no choice. Katelyn inhaled deeply, slowly released her breath, and looked Trent directly in his dark eyes.

"I need help—well, more like protection," she said quickly.

"Ok, protection is what we do," he teased. "It's in the name, after all."

Katelyn laughed nervously. "Yeah... The thing is, I need this protection as soon as possible." She clasped her hands in her lap to prevent the overwhelming need to get down on her knees and beg.

But if push came to shove, she wouldn't be averse to begging.

"Ok. Can you give me any other details at all? You know, like who and why?" His question unintentionally made Katelyn squirm in her seat. She couldn't hold his gaze any longer. Instead, she looked at her clasped hands.

"Katelyn." His deep voice caressed her name. The way he said it made it sound exotic, his accent giving it a whole new depth. Pulled by his voice, she looked up once again into his dark grey eyes. "You can trust me. I'm here to help."

Katelyn decided to keep things simple, no more facts than absolutely necessary. "My ex-boyfriend is stalking me. I managed to escape him six months ago. He's a demon and has his fingers in the paranormal black market."

Trent watched as a multitude of emotions passed over Katelyn's face. Her name echoed in the corner of his mind over and over, and he wanted to let it slide off his tongue. He was beguiled by her, and he hung on her every word. He was entranced by every look she made, every breath she took.

He didn't find her story hard to believe. The paranormal black market had become increasingly violent, more so when it became common knowledge to the rest of the world that the creatures of myth and legend did, in fact, exist. Humans now wanted paranormals, whether dead for their parts or alive as trophies, and were willing to pay big money for them. It showed clearly the shady characters that would sell their own kind for profit.

The idea, even the smallest one, that the beautiful creature in front of him was at risk of being within their grasp made his hands clench. He could feel the tell-tale signs that his own defensive guards would show if he didn't calm the inferno building inside. That worried him. His inner demon, the one he had never let loose, had awakened. Although he had always thought it would be hellbent on destruction, it surprised him with its need to protect. This female, this small, beautiful creature, had found a way to disarm his inner self, and she didn't even know it.

"Does this boyfriend—"

"*Ex*-boyfriend. He lost that right when he hit me."

"Ex," Trent corrected. "Does he know where you live?"

Trent could see the worry on her face as she nodded. "Yes. This morning, I heard them. They found my apartment. I don't know how." She hung her head, and Trent wanted nothing more than to take her in his arms. He wanted—no, *needed*—to protect her.

"Ok, so you can't go home." He watched again as she shook her head. She sniffed, and he knew without seeing that she was fighting back tears. Her confidence to start with was merely a mask, one that hid all the hurt and despair she had been dealt.

"That's fine," he answered. She pulled a tissue out of her pocket and gently wiped her eyes, before her gazed flicked up to look at him. The amber had intensified to a molten, shimmering gold, like the deep colours of a flame.

"It is?" she asked. "You can help me?"

"Yes, we can, although we have no one free to take on the job." Trent knew they had two males ready to work, but he couldn't bring himself to offer this particular job to anyone else. "That being said, I will see to this personally," he finished and watched the flare of surprise in her eyes.

"You will personally see to my safety?" Hope lit up her face. The look of near joy caused an answering thump of his heart. Its beat increased until his whole body became aware of her.

"Yes," Trent answered simply, not trusting himself to say much more. They sat there, silent but aware of each other's presence. A slow hum filled the room as the atmosphere intensified.

"Coffee!" The high-pitched voice of Margi cut through their moment, bringing them both back to the present. Trent forced a smile and reached for his cup, acutely aware of Katelyn as she did the same.

She was in his care now. She was his charge to protect. So why did he feel like a part of him needed protecting from her?

CHAPTER SEVEN

"What do you mean, she's gone?" The demon known as Duncan paced his penthouse suite. It was one of the swanky numbers that overlooked the local parkland, and in the distance he could just make out Buckingham Palace. Not that he wanted to—hell, the only reason he had wanted this suite was for its size. More room to play and let himself go. Literally.

Currently, though, he wouldn't be letting go for fun. Instead, he struggled to keep in his skin as he heard one of his subordinates inform him of how they managed to lose one small shifter who lacked any ability in self-defence. She could run— she seemed to have picked that up well enough— but she wouldn't be free for long. Six months ago, she had given him the slip, and for that alone she would get his special attention.

First, though, they needed to get her back. He had promised a lot of people the goods when he made it known that he had a phoenix in his possession, and luckily, they had been generous enough to give him some time to relocate her. Now, his time was up, and he needed her back in his possession or what he owed was coming out of his hide. Again, literally.

"I don't care how she did it," he shouted into the phone. "All I care about now is you getting her the fuck back. Now!" Hanging up, he threw the phone onto the sofa where his partner, William, sat. His long-term friend looked relaxed and at ease, even though it was both their necks on the line.

"Don't you have anything to say?" Duncan spat in Williams's direction, and was rewarded with a simple raise of an eyebrow.

"What do you want me to say? I found her to begin with. I did my part. You can't blame me if your little minions are not up to the job."

Duncan threw himself into a chair. His normal good looks—merely a show for humans—had faded to reveal a gruesome face; sunken bones covered with tight grey skin, hollowed eyes, and fangs that dripped with fetid saliva.

"Pressure getting to you a bit, I see," William joked and moved his own muscled bulk from the sofa. "We'll get her back. She's all alone in a big city. It's only a matter of time."

"That's what we don't have, William." The grotesque features slowly morphed back into the blue-eyed model as he focused on William seriously. "Time is what we are lacking."

William nodded and retrieved two crystal tumblers, both half-filled with an amber liquid, and passed one to Duncan, his face finally showing a hint of worry.

"They are coming, then."

"Yes, and if we don't have the phoenix, then it's our heads."

"Well, we had best find her, then." Both males knocked back the liquid before they made to move out of the large suite.

The hunt was on.

Suzanna sat back from her computer screen and peeked through her office window. Margi was her usual nightmarish self and about as much use as a chocolate teapot. Whatever had urged her to hire the nymph, she wasn't sure. Hell, she may have been drunk.

Suzanna frowned and squinted. Yeah she was definitely drunk. That's what you got for dealing with alpha males all day. They squabbled more than children and could pout better as well.

Shifting her neck from side to side, Suzanna sighed a little when the bones cracked, relieving some of the tension that had been housed there. Having Trent arrive had been a bloody godsend, but now she owed Hilda. She chuckled. Her friend of many years would no doubt collect when it suited her and not a moment before. It would either cost her a fortune or her pride. Either way, she owed the old trout.

Both Suzanna and Hilda didn't look as old as they were, but the banter was still the same. Names like hag and crone were usual for their relationship, but she wouldn't have it any other way. Lifting her head again, Suzanna watched as Trent led a stunning redhead into his office. Her gut instinct, along with some pesky recurring dreams, had once again proven to be right. Suzanna just hoped Trent was strong enough for what was to come.

"Margi, grab me a large coffee, will you," Suzanna shouted out, making the nymph jump and drop her nail file. Shaking her head, she focused back on her own work. Sometimes, being immortal, and a Valkyrie, had its perks.

Today was not one of them.

CHAPTER EIGHT

K atelyn stood in the doorway to Trent's flat and looked at the empty expanse. There was only a sofa present and that looked small.

"You said you flew in yesterday?" she asked quietly. She was sure he hadn't heard her until he turned and nodded.

"That's right. I haven't had a chance to get anything yet, to make it feel more like home." The way he said this caught Katelyn. It was said with such a sense of longing, one she identified with.

"I know the feeling," she admitted. "Finding somewhere to call home is harder than it looks."

Trent tilted his head as he studied her, before he nodded again and moved towards her. Gently, he took the small bag she held, and Katelyn let him. As a paranormal and a bird of legend, she kind of had an open mind about everything. Life knew how to throw, as the yanks would call them, curve balls. But what she felt in Trent's company was something she wasn't sure how to process.

The idea of soulmates had been something her kind have celebrated throughout time, along with other races. Instant love wasn't something to laugh about, and neither was the term 'mates', but she had little experience, and right now her feelings and the attitude of her bird were confusing her. She had made the mistake of trusting a male with her safety and virginity before and look where that got her. Constantly on the run.

But everything she had felt with Duncan was nothing compared to the simple feeling of protection she felt in Trent's presence. She had been petrified when she arrived at the office, yet five minutes in his company and she felt nothing more than a warmth that had started in her chest, accompanied by the now constant hum of her bird.

That warmth, though, was a sure sign of something else. Phoenixes mated for life. But how they chose their mate was what some would call, pot luck. It was a sense given to only the bird, which detected the best possible match. And as Katelyn looked at Trent, his large body moving about the apartment with ease, she realised what her bird was doing.

In times of danger, mating occurred for the protection of the species, and now her phoenix had decided that this male was it. She knew next to nothing about him, only that he was from the US and worked for the PSS. She didn't even know if he liked women. For all she knew, he could be batting for the other side. That was usually the case with gorgeous males like him.

Katelyn's heart rate spiked. What if he picked his nose? What if he hated crisp butties? This was all important information she had to know before she decided to mate, and now it looked like her bird, in her own panic, had made the choice for her.

"No... No, no, you are not doing this," she whispered as she watched the most perfect bottom encased in denim vanish from view. "Yes, he's hot, but we don't even know what he is and if he would want us. Dammit, don't do this." She spoke sternly but got nothing but louder chirps and hums in response.

"Nope, not happening," Katelyn said again. She would fight this with everything she had. The fact she had put Trent at risk was enough, and if somehow she managed to live long enough, she would make sure she wouldn't tie him to her and her hussy of a bird.

Trent walked back in, and Katelyn's mouth went dry. In that short time, he seemed bigger, his muscles more defined. His grey eyes were so dark they made her want to dive in and drown in them.

"Would you like to clean up, shower maybe? Or there's a bath? Your choice," he asked. Her eyes focused on the movement of his lips.

"Wow. Yes, please," she breathed out. "Thank you so much for this, Trent."

"It's my pleasure. Let me show you the bedroom."

"Isn't there a guest room?" Katelyn asked as her mind produced one erotic image after another of Trent barely clothed in the centre of a large bed. Her bird wasn't playing fair.

"No, sorry, it's a one-bed place. Don't worry though, I'll sleep on the couch. The bed is all yours." He smiled and moved into a large room, with a king-size bed at one end. The dark colours of the decor suited him, even if he had only been there a day. Walking past her, completely oblivious to her own inner turmoil, she heard him sigh.

Her bag had already been placed on the bed, and she walked over to it. She pulled back the zip and dug out her travel bag, which held her favourite toiletries. Made running a little easier.

When Trent came out of the bathroom, he smiled. "Have a bath and try to relax. You're safe here. Once you're ready, we can grab some food." Before he had a chance to move past her, Katelyn laid a palm on his forearm, stopping him.

She looked up into his eyes. "Thank you," she whispered.

He didn't answer, only nodded, but Katelyn hadn't missed the flare of heat in his gaze when she had touched him. Maybe...

"Trent," she called out as he reached the bedroom door. "What are you?" she asked before she could stop herself. Curiosity had won out.

Turing his head ever so slightly, he looked at her, before turning back and grabbing the door handle, ready to close the door.

"A monster." With that, he closed the door, leaving Katelyn to her thoughts. But it wasn't the word 'monster' that had her heartrate increasing again. No, it was that look in his eyes when she had touched him that told her he may not be indifferent to her touch, and maybe, just maybe, her phoenix wasn't stir crazy after all.

Maybe...

Trent closed his eyes for a second before moving away from the door to his bedroom. Why did he offer her a bath? Oh yeah, 'cause he couldn't stand being in the same room as her any longer without touching her. Since the moment she had stepped foot into his apartment, her scent had filled his senses. She managed to make his roomy apartment seem tiny, to the point he wanted to escape, just so he could draw a breath in and think.

The way his body was reacting was foreign to him. As a hybrid, normal paranormal rules didn't apply to him, or so he thought. When she touched his arm, a burning inferno had erupted through him, making him want to take her in his arms, press his lips to her own plump ones, and devour her until he had no idea where she began and he ended.

He had no idea what she was or what was hunting her, but that seemed totally irrelevant now. Trent walked into the kitchen and collected his phone, before dialling the one person who might give him some answers.

"Trent, how's bonny England?"

"Ronnie, it's glorious," Trent answered dryly, when in fact it was dull and chilly.

"Really? Isn't is usually raining? No matter, day two and already you need my help, either that or you're missing me."

"Smart, really smart. Listen, I need to ask something."

"Shoot."

"My kind... do they mate? Partner up?"

"Mmm... Trent, as you know, you are an anomaly—one of a kind. Gargoyles, for starters, were created, never born. You were. The how and why, we don't know, nor do I think we will ever know. You're best asking Taylor."

"What about my other side?" That was the side he was most nervous about. It was unpredictable and uncontrollable. Unless, it seemed, it was in the presence of Katelyn. Just the thought of her naked and in his bath made that side of him perk up again, along with his body. Trent sighed as he looked down, seeing the evidence poking out for all to see. And he wasn't a small guy by any means.

"Your other side, Trent, is as volatile as a pure

bred, but we don't know their mating rituals. Hell, we don't even know what kind you are." Trent sighed. Closing his eyes, he willed his body under control. The last thing he needed was to scare his charge with his pet iguana.

"Why do you want to know, Trent? Is there a special someone? And after only two days..." He could hear clapping, and instead of answering her question, he decided to finish the call.

"Thanks, Ronnie. Speak soon." Hanging up the phone, Trent leaned on the worktop. Ronnie was more family to him, had taken Trent in when his mother had finally lost the plot and tried to kill Trent in his sleep one day, screaming that the demons were coming. If it hadn't been for Ronnie, he didn't dare think of what he would have become.

He was no farther along now than he was before. He knew one thing, though. Whatever was hunting Katelyn, they wouldn't get to her. If anything, he was the perfect bodyguard.

He would embrace his other side to protect her.

Who would want to mess with a gargoyle/demon hybrid?

CHAPTER NINE

The bath had been exactly what Katelyn needed; a chance to stop, slow down, and think, without the worry of someone knocking her door down. It was amazing what a simple thing like having a bath could do for the soul; steady it, re-centre it, and give it focus. Only hers had taken the focus part a little too seriously.

Her bird now had one focus: Trent.

Not that she blamed her bird. He was the definition of man candy. All muscle and strength wrapped in one delicious package. She would have to be completely devoid of any of her senses to miss it. But that didn't mean she would do as her bird commanded and climb him like the proverbial tree. No, she would show some sort of decorum.

Decorum... Katelyn snorted and splashed her face with the water. Since when did she use words that sounded like that?

Trent was an enigma. She had no clue what kind of paranormal he was. Nothing gave that away, not the way he looked or dressed. Even his demeanour gave no clue. His scent was different but not unpleasant. It reminded her of a stormy summer's day, the smell of rain in the air mixed in with something that was so uniquely Trent she wanted to bottle it, spray it on a cushion and cuddle it constantly. She would have said cuddle him, but that was the bird talking.

Removing Trent from her thoughts was easier said than done, so she instead moved her thoughts to her ex, Duncan, the definition of arsehole with an extra twat thrown in for good measure. If she'd had any inkling that he was a demon, she would have steered clear. Even when she told him what she was, he had taken it with almost no surprise.

Katelyn shuddered at the memory of what had happened. His touch had once been pleasurable but now only made her feel queasy. She had given in to him far too easily, and she regretted it. It was like a stain she couldn't remove. A tattoo on her soul.

Katelyn stood in the vast tub and gingerly stepped out, pulling on the thick robe Trent had left out for her. She couldn't help but sniff the collar, hoping to find his scent on it, but was disappointed to find it held only the smell of the softener that had been used to clean it.

After wrapping the belt around her waist, Katelyn slowly unbraided her hair. It was slightly damp from the moisture in the air. As the heavy weight dropped, she ran her fingers through the long locks. If only life was as peaceful as it was at that precise moment. But no, not for her. Even her hair was a wanted commodity for those in the black market. Everything on a phoenix could be sold. Dead, her corpse could be dismembered, and a huge profit made, but alive... Well, alive she was a constant donor.

After she escaped from Duncan, she had taken the time to research what was hunting her. For the regular human, Google wouldn't bring up much, but after she had spoken to the others on Ashes.com, they had shown her how to access the dark side of the net. For paranormals, that is.

A whole new, dark world had unravelled before her, and her eyes had been opened. In short, Katelyn had found out she was worth at least half a million pounds. That was if they could only harvest her the once.

Katelyn shuddered as a cold tingle travelled the length of her spine. *Harvest.* It made it sound so mundane, when it was the complete opposite. To be harvested meant every part of her physical being would be collected and sold. Her hair, her tears, blood, eggs... the list went on. They were the ultimate key to become indestructible. A way of being able to heal from any wounds or ailments, a way to survive anything. Katelyn now understood a little of what drove Duncan to hunt her down.

Only she wasn't the meek, quiet bird who had escaped. No, she had tasted what it felt like to be free. She had sampled the delights of independence, even if it was for a short time, and Katelyn would not give it up. Not for Duncan, not for anyone.

Picking up her discarded clothes, Katelyn threw open the bathroom door, only to walk into a large, hard, and very naked chest.

"Oof," Katelyn mumbled against Trent's skin, her hands pressed against his well-defined abs as she tried to find her equilibrium. She had little fear of falling as she felt Trent's hands cup her shoulders. Katelyn felt her face go the same colour as her hair as she tipped her head back to look up at him.

"You ok?" he asked, and Katelyn blinked slowly. The nearness of such a male specimen was messing with her brain. What did he say?

"Katelyn? Everything ok? I was just going to knock to see how you were doing and to ask if you were hungry."

Katelyn blinked and nodded slowly. Pushing away from his chest, she moved back. "Yes. Sorry, you just surprised me." She smiled and pulled the robe tighter around her. The humming had started up again, so loud in her head she was positive Trent could hear it. The urge to tell her bird to shut the hell up was tempting to give in to, but she didn't want to have to explain why she was reprimanding her other side. That would only open up one huge can of worms, ones she wasn't ready to release. She smiled shyly.

"So... food?" she asked as she stepped around Trent. Trying to ignore all the strange and new feelings he and her damn bird were creating, she walked over to her bag and pulled out a worn pair of jeans, a t-shirt, and underwear, before looking back at the large male. His back was even more impressive than his front. There was not one inch of fat.

Katelyn had to quickly avert her eyes as he turned. The last thing she needed was Trent clocking her whilst she was gawping.

"What would you like?" Trent asked and moved to a chest of drawers on the other side of the room. His movements were swift as he pulled another plain black t-shirt from the top draw and covered all that muscle Katelyn had been perving on.

"I don't mind," Katelyn answered.

"You decide what you want, and when I come back, we can order it." Slowly, he approached with a pad and pen. She had failed to notice he had them before. "I need you to write down your address for me, see if we can catch who is stalking you."

Katelyn took the pad from him. Turning, she leaned on the chest of drawers and quickly wrote down her address, along with the alarm code. "Will they be able to grab me some clothes?" she asked as she handed back the pad, then wrapped her arms around herself once again.

"Of course. Whatever you need." Trent's voice once again sent a shiver down her spine, its deep gruffness making her bird chirp, and if Katelyn didn't watch herself, she would find herself joining it.

"Thank you," Katelyn called out as Trent moved to the door. His hand reached out to grab the handle, but he turned his head, showing the small smile that creased his mouth.

"My pleasure... Katelyn." The sound of her name on his lips made her tremble, but it was his smile that made her knees go weak. Full lips gave her glimpses of perfect white teeth, all completed with dimples she had no doubt had broken hearts.

Katelyn just about held herself upright, until Trent shut the door behind him. Her knees gave out and she landed hard on the bed.

"Damn." Katelyn fanned her face and giggled. "That right there is one hunk of a man." The chirp, followed by the loud hum in her head, signalled her bird's agreement. Katelyn smiled. Since Duncan, her bird had been intermittent with her communication. Only talking when they were safe. Only now she had become quiet again, but for a different reason. Her bird liked Trent... really liked him. She was keeping quiet to help Katelyn.

Trent closed the door behind him, and the smile he had given Katelyn turned into a grin. His hearing hadn't missed the small sigh she had released. He hadn't missed the flushed cheeks either. His ego grew, knowing it had been him to cause that reaction. He wanted to puff up his chest like a silverback. He had always known he looked good, but it was now he really appreciated it.

The feelings his new charge was stirring within him, worried him. It felt too soon and far too fast. Trent collected his cell from the kitchen counter and immediately started scrolling through his contacts. As soon as he found the number he needed, he hit the call button and brought the phone to his ear.

Three rings later and a similar deep voice to his own answered sleepily. "Trent... I had a feeling you would call."

"Really? And what, or should I say who, gave you that idea, Tay?" Trent answered his friend. Taylor was one half of the duo that made up his mated friends. Ronnie had lucked out when she met Taylor. What better protection than a gargoyle? But he should have known Ronnie would blab. She couldn't keep anything from that mate of hers.

"Oh, just a gut instinct, and Ronnie may have said something." Tiredness had been replaced by humour and the sound of rustling sheets. Shit, he had forgotten the time difference.

"What do you need to know, Trent?" Taylor's voice turned serious, and for once, Trent was glad. Tay was the least serious out of the couple and usually would be the one to crack the jokes.

"Information," Trent stated simply, gaining a sigh on the end of the line.

"Go on then. I'm all ears."

Trent had made his way out of the apartment and into the hallway, only now he stopped partway down the corridor. Leaning back against the wall, he thought quickly on what to say. This was difficult for him. He was a private man. Not many people knew what he was, and even fewer knew how he felt. But he needed answers, or a way to get them.

"Trent, come on, man, out with it before I put the phone down and go back to grabbing my mate's ass," Taylor grumbled, giving Trent the push he needed.

"About that... about your mate," Trent started.

"Be careful what you say from now on, Trent,

especially about my wife." Taylor's voice had shot from playful to deadly in seconds.

"No, wait," Trent answered quickly, "it's not like that. I want to know... What did you feel when you first saw her?" Trent shot out, scrubbing a large hand down his face. His heart rate had picked up, and he felt sweat beading on his forehead. Why was it so damn hard to discuss this stuff?

"Ahhh," was all the answer he got from Taylor, before silence, then the rustle of sheets filled the line, followed by the mumbled words, *"Shh, baby, go back to sleep. I'll be back in a minute."* Trent clenched his fists as impatience filled him.

Taylor's voice filled the line again. "When I first saw her, it was like a punch to the gut. Just looking at her, there was an instant attraction. But, man, once I had spoken to her, I wanted nothing more than to get my hands on her."

Trent unclenched his hands and listened carefully.

"You know how small she is, and how she likes to walk around like she's nine feet tall and can take on anyone?" Taylor didn't wait for an answer. "Well, that caused every protective bone in my body to wake up and go on high alert. It was different from when I was—sorry, when *we* were cursed. There was no forcing me. This was a need a hundred times more powerful, and still is. It annoys the shit out of her." Taylor paused, and somehow, Trent could tell he was smiling "Then throw in the instantaneous, almost overwhelming lust... Well, that *maybe* gives you a hint of what it would feel like."

Trent blew out a breath. "And now?"

Taylor laughed. "And now..." he sighed. "Now, I would move heaven and earth for her. She is my mate, and she was from that first moment."

Trent was silent for a moment, processing every word Taylor had said. Every one of them had hit home.

"Listen, man, whoever it is that has your wires all scrambled, I'm glad."

"What?" Trent answered, a little shocked. He wasn't happy about feeling the way he did. It was like his equilibrium had malfunctioned.

"You've been alone for far too long. If this female is making you feel even a portion of what I described, then she's yours. It's that simple. We gargoyles are that simple. It doesn't matter if she's human or para, all that matters is—"

Taylor stopped midsentence. Trent stood straighter and moved away from the wall, his phone gripped in his hand. What if his friend was in trouble? He couldn't help from another country.

Mumbled noises filled the line, and Trent moved the phone from his ear. Worry soon turned to humour as he heard a feminine moan. Trent shook his head as he disconnected the call and shoved the phone back into his jeans pocket. Taylor and Ronnie were lucky bastards, but he wouldn't begrudge them their happiness. They deserved it tenfold.

Heading for the elevator, Trent mentally made a plan, one that included trying his hand at romancing the beautiful Katelyn. He would do as Taylor suggested and follow his instincts.

And right now, every one of them screamed that the little firebird in his apartment was his.

"Mine," he growled as he stepped into the elevator and pushed the button for the ground floor.

She would be; she just didn't know it yet.

CHAPTER TEN

As far as Trent was concerned, he had been away from his apartment and Katelyn for far too long. The jobs he wanted to get done had taken longer than he anticipated. So far, he had sent one of the wolves on staff to scout out Katelyn's home. Only persuading that wolf hadn't been easy.

It was looking like he wasn't the only one to have 'women issues', but Mike had complied—after he got some personal issues off his chest and gave Trent some advice he never asked for—and left with instructions to grab her stuff as requested and see if anyone was lurking about.

He had also needed to let Suzanna know about his new charge, or job—whatever she wanted to call it—though she hadn't been that surprised. That being said, Suzanna and Hilda were long distance besties who constantly texted each other. He had also found out from the nymph that Suzanna had a thing for interfering, though she referred to it as matchmaking any of the single males. Mike had been set up on a multitude of dates.

Grabbing his phone from the desk, he made his way out of his still empty office. He made sure to close the door before moving swiftly towards the elevator, eager to get back to his apartment. The need was quickly turning into a full-blown itch, one that demanded a certain redhead to scratch. The thought of her small delicate hands on him were enough to bring a small moan to his lips and make his cock to go from disinterested to full blown, *I'm ready. Let's do this,* in a matter of seconds.

"Well, there's the lust," Trent admitted out loud, thinking back over Taylor's words. In a matter of less than twenty-four hours, Katelyn had managed to not only gain his help, but she had also gotten so far under his skin even surgery wouldn't help. Not that he wanted it to. The feelings running riot in his system were new, and yes, they were scary, but he wouldn't want them to change.

As the elevator pinged open, Trent thought over his plan. The wooing, as Mike had called it, would have to wait. Above everything else, Katelyn's safety came first. The protection of an innocent was something every gargoyle made, cursed or born had ingrained into their very soul. The fact the innocent party was, simply put, his mate, made the feelings a hell of a lot stronger. The need to go all caveman and take her away, lock her up so only he could protect, feed, and do other more pleasurable things, was pushing against his skin, making his other self ripple on the surface. Both sides of him, instead of fighting for dominance, now had one solo focus: Katelyn.

Trent was not quite sure he wanted her to see that side of him just yet, especially when he had no idea what kind of para she was. All he knew was that she was his.

His little firebird.

As Trent reached for the door to the apartment, he stopped. He had not one single clue how to proceed. Hell, give him vampires gone rogue, pixies swarming, even a werewolf gone crazy, but this... on this he had drawn a total blank.

His palms felt clammy, sweat beaded again on his forehead and up his spine, and his stomach rolled. What if she didn't like him? She liked the way he looked—he definitely hadn't missed the heated glances she threw his way when he removed his shirt. Only, he was still unsure.

Trent wasn't a virgin. He had certainly had his fair share of lovers in the past. Getting them hadn't been difficult. But all they had been was a hook-up. They never cared what was behind the good looks and solid muscle. Most did it for the bragging rights—*I did it with a para.* Yes, he had agreed to it. His very half-breed nature meant he was a sexual being. His demon had always craved release, up until recently. Right now, it craved more.

So did he.

Trent pushed through the door of the apartment and walked into the open-plan lounge, the view now giving him a stunning sunset of reds, golds and oranges. The colour of flame. And sat before it was Katelyn, curled up on the sofa.

Her curvy form sat bathed in flame. Her long hair, now loose from its braid, cascaded in thick locks over her shoulder. Trent was transfixed. He paused mid-step, just to watch her as she toyed with a strand of hair, braiding and loosening it as she looked out over London. Keeping his steps quiet, he moved towards the sofa. She was a pull, a tug, and one he wouldn't deny.

"Hey," he called out quietly, not wanting to scare her. He expected her to jump, only she surprised him by simply turning her head towards him and smiling.

Damn, that smile hit Trent in two places, almost like a well-judged combination punch. One straight to the groin, the other to his gut. Her lips taunted him, called to him and urged him to take a taste. See if they tasted as good as they looked. But her eyes... the amber seemed to blaze with fire like an Australian opal when turned into the light. Flames danced in their depths, beguiling him, and it was only her husky words that saved him from drowning.

"How did it go?" Her voice whispered over his skin, and the hairs on the back of his neck rose in response. Pulling himself together, Trent focused on the reason she was here in the first place.

"I'm waiting to hear back from the operative we sent," he admitted. "Once he's back, we'll have an idea of how to proceed."

"Will he be safe? I don't want anyone hurt because of me." Her face pinched with worry. Trent was surprised by her question but became distracted as she started to chew on her lower lip. Trent watched as the plump flesh became swollen from her ministrations.

He fought the urge to taker her chin in his hand and stop her assault, instead he answered, "It's ok, Katelyn. It's our job. His job. Mike is more than capable of looking after himself."

He smiled at her and let himself reach out to take her hand in his own. The size difference between the two was startling but made his protective instincts kick into a higher gear.

"I will keep you safe," he vowed. Katelyn nodded in response but said nothing. Instead, she looked down at their joined hands. Slowly, so not to startle her, he moved his palm, so it was face up and laid it on her lap. Her fingers instantly whispered over his hand, her soft touch a pleasurable contrast to his own callused skin.

Katelyn traced each line, and every touch only served to ignite him inside. Trent felt the atmosphere change with each sweep of her finger. Static filled the air, and Trent's body reacted. His breathing increased as his blood pounded through his veins. Lust in its purest form coursed through him. Trent lifted his gaze from their hands to study Katelyn's face, only to find her amber eyes watching him. Only this time, it wasn't the sunset causing flames to dance in their fiery depths. Her own breathing had increased, her chest rising and falling quickly.

Her voice was throaty, and with each syllable said, his cock twitched in answer. "Do you feel that?"

Trent couldn't answer. His mouth had gone dry. He moved his tongue from behind his teeth and swept it across his lips.

He felt it alright, and so did his cock.

He fought the urge to close the small gap between them and take her mouth with his own, mastering her in the best possible way, stamping himself on her very soul. His hand folded around hers, ready to pull her into his arms. Ready to see if that look in her eye really was for him. But common sense resumed at the ringing of his phone.

Whatever spell had been cast vanished in an instant, and Trent felt its loss. Reluctantly, he released her hand. Her cheeks flushed bright red as she looked up at him, but then she turned away.

Trent sighed as he pulled his phone from his pocket and answered. "Mike. What have you got?"

Oh my god! Oh my god!

Katlyn turned her face away from Trent, her cheeks burning as she struggled to take in a deep breath. She had never in her life found being in a room with a male difficult before, but with Trent, everything she had previously experienced was wrong. The sexual tension had been so thick the hairs on her arms had risen to attention. His touch had set her on fire, and not in the traditional sense for her kind. The feel of him under her fingers had ignited something deep inside, like her phoenix had finally unfurled her wings and was ready to fly.

When Trent left to go to work, she had sat down and thought long and hard about how she felt. In the absence of his distracting presence, she had processed every feeling she had encountered since their meeting. She would have liked to have spoken to her parents about him, but the last thing she needed at this point was their intervention or to put them in danger.

If she really thought about it, she needed to focus on her current situation, the one where she survives long enough to contemplate having a relationship. Her phoenix had made the choice for her,

but she just couldn't follow that blindly.
Could she?

For starters, Katelyn knew nothing about Trent
other than he was American and worked for the
PSS. She needed to know more. Maybe that was
the first step.

Her gaze tracked him—all six feet plus of him
—as he moved about the room whilst he talked on
the phone. Usually, someone as large as him would
lumber, but not Trent. No, he stalked, and he did it
quietly. Katelyn watched each and every muscle
bunch under the t-shirt he wore, and she flushed as
she remembered him without it.

Physically he was perfect—to her. Attraction
wasn't a problem. She would quite happily make
like a pole dancer and climb him like a pole. But she
wanted more than that. More than just instant lust.

Trent wasn't the type she usually went for. Yes,
her ex had been ripped, but in a leaner way, and he
was nowhere near as tall as Trent. Only now...

Now Trent was all she thought of and had
been since the moment he came to her outside his
office. His words pulled her from her inner
musings.

"Right. Anything else?" he asked into the

phone. Nodding once, he ended the call and looked at the screen for a moment before putting it away. Slowly, he moved back towards her and sat down like he had before, but instead of just sitting there, he took both her hands in his own, squeezing gently before running his thumbs over the pulse points on her wrists. His voice pulled her gaze from their hands and to his stormy grey eyes.

"Mike will be delivering your bag with what you've asked for tomorrow. Your apartment building is being watched and they are tracking anyone that looks out of the ordinary. So he's having to wait for the cover of night to go in."

"But how will he get in? How will he avoid being seen?" she asked, now feeling the worry of being stalked set back in. She was putting others in danger for her, but she didn't have the courage to go it alone.

"He has certain skills, Katelyn. Mike's a pro, and he will get you what you want from the apartment."

Really, did he honestly think all she cared about were her things? She wasn't that shallow.

"I don't care about my things, Trent. I don't want anyone to get hurt," she snapped. Trent said nothing, but the widening of his eyes was the telling sign that she had surprised him.

"Mike will be fine. In fact, he loves to play the covert role." Trent chuckled in an attempt to lighten the mood. "But what I do need right now is for you to tell me more about those following you."

Katelyn pulled her gaze away and returned to staring at their joined hands. Keeping what she was a secret was getting more and more difficult. She wanted nothing more than to trust Trent with that knowledge. But...

One of Trent's hands moved. His finger hooked under her chin and pulled her face upwards until their gazes clashed again. He moved closer, and Katelyn forgot how to breathe.

His face—his lips—were less than an inch away.

"You can trust me, Katelyn." The words were a deep grumble before he gently pressed his lips to hers. The touch made her gasp, but Trent kept the touch light, coaxing her to kiss him back. She did, slowly at first, his taste her new addiction. But all too soon, he pulled away.

"Talk to me," he beseeched her, only Katelyn couldn't tell him. She needed something. Something that proved she could trust him.

"I will. But..." she started.

"But?" he urged.

"I need something from you. Please," she almost pleaded. "Tell me what you are." She lifted her eyes to his, pleased to see he hadn't moved away. In fact, he was closer, so close Katelyn could feel the heat from his body and inhale the scent from his skin.

"I already told you, little one."

"No, you didn't," Katelyn argued back. "Simply stating you are a monster is not telling me, and it's not the type of thing you say when trying to get someone to trust you, is it?"

She watched as he searched her face. She knew she looked flushed from his surprise kiss, but she also knew he was searching for something else.

"I'm positive the only monster I have met is the one stalking me," she added and felt the hand wrapped around her own tighten, before he released her. Disappointment filled her, until she looked down to find his hand palm up on her lap.

She looked again at the size difference between hers and his. It should have scared her. In fact, it did the opposite.

It comforted her.

Only now, his usually tanned skin was changing. The softness she had felt before slowly hardened. Scales became apparent on the surface, and his knuckled had doubled in size. Trent's fingernails elongated, becoming long, lethal-looking talons.

Katelyn gasped but couldn't look away. Instead of dropping his hand, she turned it over. It felt heavier than before, but she became mesmerised by the way the light reflected from the hardened skin. Thinking back to her studies as a child, she remembered how her parents had told her stories about many of the para races, telling her the ones that would, if needed, help a phoenix, and the ones that would harm. She wracked her brains until one word popped into her head and stayed there.

Lifting her eyes, she met Trent's grey ones. Worry etched his brow, and with no thought, she reached up to smooth the wrinkle.

"I know what you are," she said with a smile.

"Then say it, Katelyn," he answered, his half shift making his voice deeper and rougher.

"Gargoyle," she whispered, before she leaned back in and pressed her lips to his.

CHAPTER ELEVEN

Katelyn's reaction to knowing what he was definitely wasn't the one he was expecting, but the one he was getting now was a damn sight better than screaming and running away. Yes, she had guessed right, even if only in part, but he would tell her after she stopped kissing him of his other half.

But right now, he was struggling to focus on anything that wasn't Katelyn's soft lips and intoxicating taste. He let her control the kiss, allowing her to get used to the size of his presence, and to be honest, he enjoyed giving up the control, even when everything in him screamed to push onto her back and explore every single inch of skin. He satisfied himself with gripping her hips in his large hands. His little firebird was now on her knees on the couch, her hands on his shoulders, nails digging in as she took her time tasting him.

By the gods she was amazing. Her taste reminded him of strawberries and roasted marshmallows. Both he adored. Moving his hands, he memorized each and every curve, until he had her encased within his arms. Unable to hold himself back, he pulled her close, pressing her small frame to his. Chest to chest, he plundered the expanse of her mouth. Taking back control, his thrust his tongue, duelling with her own for dominance. The moment he gained it was a small victory, one that was signalled with a throaty moan. The sound made his already hard cock like granite, pressing against the fly of his jeans.

If her simple moan could unman him like a youth, Trent was curious what his touch on her bare skin could do. Pulling her tighter to him, he pushed his large hands under her t-shirt, feeling her soft, bare skin against his palms, and he growled into her mouth. Higher they travelled until they hit the strap of her bra. He made quick work of the small fastening, unsnapping it without pause, before he kept one hand on her back, cradling her to him, and the other went on a mission.

Breasts made for his hands alone is what he found as his palm skated over one, her nipple pebbling instantly. The calluses on his palm caught the peak and made Katelyn moan again.

Trent found he was addicted to not only her taste but the sounds she made. He wanted them all to be because of him. Her pleasure was his, and he found both his gargoyle and the demon locked deep inside wanted it as well. Taking the nipple between his thumb and finger, Trent squeezed and pulled, tugging on it.

"Oh god." He smiled as Katelyn broke the kiss, burying her head into the crook of his neck. Her whispered breaths feathered over his skin. With his hand on her back, he pulled her closer, giving her no choice but to straddle the thigh he had on the couch. Her groan of pleasure was nearly his undoing as her jean clad, heated core sat over his thigh.

Still he continued to play with her nipple, loving each and every sound she made as he coerced it into a tight nub. He itched to bend his head and take it in his mouth but settled for moving to the other and giving it the same treatment. Katelyn's mews of delight urged him on, her own body lost to the pleasure as she moved her hips against his thigh.

In a small part of his brain, Trent had doubts, thoughts of whether he was taking advantage of Katelyn, that this was all happening too quickly. Freeing his hands, he moved them to cup her face so he could look into her eyes. The last thing he ever wanted was for her to hate him.

"Katelyn," he cooed and smirked as she opened her eyes. The desire in their depths made the amber spark like a fire was being lit.

"Katelyn." He whispered her name and waited for her eyes to focus on him.

"What's wrong?" her lust-filled voice asked. The husky tone had Trent tightening his hold. "Why did you stop?"

"Baby." His thumbs stroked her cheeks. "I stopped because I shouldn't be taking advantage of you," he admitted. He didn't want to stop. Hell, he would be happy to be locked up with her for endless days, learning her body. Memorising it.

"Trent," she breathed out, her eyes focused solely on his lips. He couldn't help but smile.

"Yeah, baby." He gently pushed a lock of her

hair from her face, the silk strands curling around his fingers.

"Make me forget," she whispered as she moved her mouth closer. "Please, don't stop," she almost begged, and Trent was lost. How could he deny her?

Without saying another word, Trent took control of her lips. She didn't want him to stop, so he wouldn't, and he would damn well make her forget about her ex. He would brand himself on her.

Pushing his thigh against her, he thrust his tongue into her mouth, and she moaned loudly. He wanted to make her come, needed to hear her lose control. His hands drifted back to her breasts, pushing her top and bra up and out of the way so he could have unlimited access. Taking the peaks within his fingers, he tugged again, and was rewarded by a long, low moan. Katelyn's body thrusted against his thigh as he pushed up, letting her ride him.

He was desperate to get them skin to skin, with nothing between them, but that would have to wait. Katelyn needed release, and he would give it to her. Pulling again on her nipples as he thrusted his muscled thigh against her damp core, he plundered her mouth.

He wanted her release, needed it.

"Come for me, baby," he growled against her lips as he twisted her nipples and thrust upward. His reward was instantaneous as Katelyn erupted. Her cries were swallowed as he continued to take her mouth with brutal passion. His hands gentled upon her breasts, cupping them, massaging them as she rode out her orgasm. His kisses slowly became little nibbles on her lips as their breaths mingled, and the storm calmed.

There was nothing sexier than watching a woman come, nothing sexier than watching *his* woman come because of him.

His. She was his.

That thought didn't shock him as much as he thought it would. Trent had been searching his whole life for a home, a place to belong. He just never realised that maybe he had been looking at it all wrong from the start.

Home for him wasn't a place, it was a woman.

A strong, beautiful redhead who called to his monster instead of running from it.

Yes, Katelyn was his.

CHAPTER TWELVE

Katelyn had lost the ability to speak, that and the ability to form any sort of coherent thought had gone, vanished as soon as that orgasm had ripped through her, taking with it any doubt that this man was her mate. Her bird had chosen, and she now agreed.

Hell, any guy who could give a girl release from a bit of tug play on her nipples was one up on the game. But Trent was different, and not just in the para sort of way. She felt safe around him; her bird felt safe around him. He thought himself a monster, but he was far from it.

Katelyn rested her head on his shoulder, trying to catch her breath, which was harder than it sounded. Her lungs felt on fire, on par to how she guessed it would feel to run a marathon. Her body hummed with pleasure, one she was eager to experience again. If Trent could send her shooting for the stratosphere just by touching her breasts, then what would happen if they made love?

Katelyn felt her core clench at the thought. Her ex had been her only experience, and already Trent had blown that out of the water. Her bird had stopped her strange yet comforting purring and now made no sound. Instead, all Katelyn could feel was a deep-seated contentment. It started deep down in the depths of her soul, deep in that place where her bird resided. Trent, in twenty-four hours, had filled a hole she hadn't realised was empty.

"Katelyn?" His voice sounded in her ear, its husky edge making her lips twitch. Slowly, she lifted her face. His dark eyes met hers and the heat contained in the orbs sent shivers up and down her spine.

"Are you ok?" he questioned. "I didn't hurt you, did I?" The tone of his voice was laced with worry. That simple act of caring pulled at Katelyn's heart. This male, this huge, sexy male, was concerned about her, worried he had hurt her when he had, in fact, done the opposite and given her the most pleasure she had ever felt in her life. Not only that, but as she sat perched on his lap, she could feel his own arousal, and yet he did nothing about it, only caring about her. Katelyn couldn't help the sigh that fell from her lips.

"Katelyn?" Trent asked again, using his large hand to cup her cheek and pull her face gently to look up at him. She hadn't realised she had looked away. In doing so, she had caused Trent to worry. She hated that look in his eyes and wanted it gone.

"I'm fine," she whispered and smiled up at him. "More than fine." She widened her smile as she moved her hands to his shoulders. Pushing up so she could move her legs, she lifted one over his lap, so instead of being side saddle, she was now straddling his hips. As soon as her core met his arousal, they both moaned, the contact sending electric currents through Katelyn's body.

Katelyn would show Trent how she felt; show him he hadn't done anything to hurt her. She would take the worry that was in his eyes and give him something else to think about. With a grin, Katelyn sealed her lips over his as she wrapped her arms around his neck, seating herself fully against him.

It was time for Katelyn to take charge.

Mike stood, his body hidden deep within the shadow. He called to them, pulling them close around him. His unique skill of being able to hide his presence had come in handy on more than one occasion and had saved his hide as well.

The information Trent had given him was minimal, but he had worked with less. His simple job of watching the client's house and, if possible, gaining entry for some clothes could be seen as an insult to his skill. But Trent seemed like a nice enough bloke, considering he had only met him the day before. He had to give it to the man, he took the heat off him when Suzanna was up to her matchmaking tricks again. For that he would do the recon needed. Besides, it kept him out of trouble. By trouble he meant stalking a particularly beautiful human who had no idea he existed.

Mike sighed. That was a dilemma for another day.

Cracking his neck, Mike focused on the building on the other side of the road. An older building, it had those metal steps that lead up to the outside as a fire escape. Its main door was keycode activated, but he wouldn't be able to use that. Not when the only way he was going to be able to enter the building would be in his shifter form. Well, that what was he had been told to do; keep out of sight and avoid being seen.

The building was being watched. He had spotted at least three men lurking, one in a brand spanking new BMW, which, in itself, gave the game away. No one in the crack end of London would have a car like that and park it without a bodyguard.

The other two were stood having a fag against the wall a few meters down from the building—again, stealth was obviously new to them. Dressed in expensive suits, they looked more out of place than the BMW.

Mike tilted his head as he watched them, and his plan to go in shifted changed. These boys were amateurs, and he wondered if they knew their arse from their elbow. Releasing the shadows, he casually walked out of the alley, hands deep in his pockets. Mike would try the innocent look, which, for a six-feet-seven shifter, was easier said than done.

As expected, the men eyed him briefly before quickly ignoring him. In seconds, Mike had gained access to the building and was heading up the stairs. He took them two at a time and was soon in front of the address Trent had given him. His new boss hadn't said much, only to get in, grab some items for his charge, scope out who and what was watching the place, before making it back. Mike tilted his head and listened as his hand touched the doorknob of the flat. His instincts, ones that had saved his life on more than one occasion, flared, giving him seconds to duck before a spray of bullets peppered the door right where he was standing.

Mike was thankful for his shifter speed. Without that, he would be making like a sieve on the floor, all holy and such. Keeping in a crouched position, he moved backwards along the landing, eyes focused on the direction from where the bullets had come. Whoever was watching the flat meant business, and whatever that girl had, they were not messing about.

"Come out! We have you surrounded."

The deep voice and its command made Mike roll his eyes. It was almost too cliché. Instead of answering, he kept quiet and kept moving. He needed to find the fire escape. They had guns; he didn't. It was that simple. Yes, he could quite easily rip their throats out through their arsehole if he so wished, but he couldn't do it when being shot at. Best he make an escape and regroup with Trent.

"Come out! We know what you are," the voice called again. His next words stopped Mike short. "All we want is the girl. Tell us where she is, and we will let you out of here unharmed."

Mike snorted this time, its sound echoing off the walls of the landing. So Trent's charge wasn't hiding something. She *was* the something, a paranormal more wanted on the black market than anything else on the planet. Mike also knew, from an unfortunate personal experience, what the bastards would do if they got their hands on her.

Standing slowly, Mike made his choice. He needed out, and he would have to go through them to do it. He needed to warn Trent. Not bothering to remove his clothes, Mike shifted, letting his wolf out. The sound of cracking bones as they realigned was followed by the deep snarls of his wolf.

Letting off a deep howl, Mike shot forward, the speed of his wolf greater than his own. He ignored the burn as bullets ripped into his hide, even the idiot that decided his body could stop a hundred and fifty pound wolf. Screams echoed behind Mike as he ploughed through the body again, ignoring the burn that now travelled up his flank. Normal bullets couldn't cause that. Mike gritted his teeth. The bastards had used silver.

Fresh air hit his face as he smashed through the window, the sound of gunfire following him into the night.

CHAPTER THIRTEEN

Trent growled low as Katelyn changed her position on his lap. As soon as she straddled him, he couldn't help the groan of need that left his lips, her heated core right there next to his cock that was punching its way through his jeans. The zip would no doubt leave a permanent impression if he didn't release it soon. But he wouldn't, not yet.

As Katelyn took control, he relaxed back into the sofa and let her. Wrapping his arms around her waist, he gave the reins to her, letting her dictate the pace. Hell, he would agree to anything for her as long as she kept kissing him like she was.

Her taste exploded on his tongue, and he drank her in. He felt like he had been dying of thirst and she was his first sip of water. The demons he fought deep inside now responded to her touch, but instead of being at odds with each other, they were now one. One goal, one aim. This woman in his arms, in a matter of hours, had become the centre of his universe.

Trent growled again as she ground her core against his cock. Pleasure, like nothing he had felt before, poured through him, making him buck his own hips in response. Katelyn had gone from shy and scared to a firebird at his touch, and didn't that just feed his ego. He had always thought of himself as a bumbling giant, yet Katelyn made him feel different.

He felt strong and powerful. He would protect her. It was that simple. She was his life now. She was his everything.

Trent slowly slid his hands up her back, pushing the fabric out of the way as he went, needing to feel her bare skin; skin that felt so soft, almost like the petals of a flower. Later, he would kiss every inch of her, love her with his mouth so she knew who she now belonged to. He would claim Katelyn both in the ways of mortals and in the ways of his people, both gargoyle and his other side. He would mark her and love her.

Trent could feel the change as it flowed

through him but could do little to stop it. His tanned skin became grey stone, clothing ripped as he doubled in size, making Trent feel a little like the big green dude from the movies. Katelyn gasped, her kisses stopping as she looked down at him.

"Oh, wow," she breathed out, and moved her hands to touch him, pushing the ripped material of his t-shirt out of the way. Fingers pressed and swept over his stone skin, yet there was no fear, only admiration. A part of Trent was ashamed he had been so out of control that he turned, but as Katelyn looked at him with nothing but affection, he couldn't help but puff up his large chest.

"You are no monster, Trent," she breathed out and bent her head, laying a small kiss over a solid pec, right over his heart. "Far from it," she whispered.

Surprising him again, she pushed up on his lap and pressed her soft lips to his cold, hard ones. An action that melted him. The change reversed itself, stone changing back to flesh as he wrapped his arms around her and pressed her to him, chest to chest as he took over the kiss.

His tongue slid into the hot crevice of her mouth and marked every inch of it before it duelled with her own. He wanted Katelyn—no, *needed* her, with a desperation he had never felt before. Her body melded against his as their groans of pleasure filled the room. He wanted her, yet he was worried about scaring her away, Hell, he burned for her.

"I—" Trent started as he reluctantly pulled his mouth away from hers, instead kissing down her neck. He growled as she tipped her head back, giving him better access. Her hands delved into his short hair, holding him to her. There was nowhere else he would rather be right now.

"Katelyn," he breathed against her skin, biting down slightly where her neck met her shoulder. There was so much he wanted to say, so much he wanted to tell her.

"Katelyn, I—" he began again.

BANG, BANG, BANG!

Trent leapt to his feet at the sound of fists on the door, his arms still wrapped tight around Katelyn as he moved slowly around the sofa. Gently sliding Katelyn down his body, he pushed her towards his bedroom.

"Go into the bathroom and lock the door. Don't come out until I come for you."

"But—" Trent stopped her before she could

argue, his lips pressing hard against hers, before he pushed her away.

"No buts, Katelyn. Do as I say."

BANG, BANG, BANG!

Trent kept his eyes on the door but listened as Katelyn moved through his room. He waited until he heard the lock of the bathroom door before he moved forward. Trent let the change affect his hands. Claws erupted from his nail beds, sharp and lethal. Without waiting for another knock, he threw open the solid wooden door.

"Fuck, Mike," Trent cursed as the werewolf slumped into the hallway, his right arm gripping his side as blood leaked through his fingers.

"What the hell happened?" Trent pulled the wolf into the hallway and slammed the door shut. Gently, so as not to hurt the male, Trent lifted him up and walked him towards the sofa. The sofa where, only moments ago, he had been loving on his woman. Trent couldn't fight the smirk that lifted his lips.

"Err, Trent," Mike called, and Trent shook his head and lowered the wolf onto the leather. "Thanks and all, mate, but I don't like you that way," the wolf coughed out and nodded towards

Trent, who was still sporting a hard on from his time with Katelyn.

"It ain't for you, Mike," Trent growled out, not in the least embarrassed. "Now, tell me what happened."

"Yeah, I will, but you gotta help me get this fucking thing out of me. It's burning like a mother fucker. The bastards shot me with silver." Trent watched as Mike rolled to his side, revealing the large entry wound under his ribs. Hell, the mutt was lucky to still be breathing, never mind walking.

"Only one?" Trent questioned as he helped the werewolf onto the sofa

Mike nodded. "Yeah, the others went straight through. Still fucking hurt though." He grimaced, his body bowing in pain as the silver took effect on his body.

Nodding, Trent left Mike on the sofa and moved back towards his bedroom. He needed towels, and he would need Katelyn's help. There was no way he would be able to dig the bullet out with his giant-sized paws.

Knocking on the bathroom door, he called her name.

"Katelyn, it's me. Ope—*oomph*." No sooner had he said her name than the door was thrown open and she was back in his arms, her own wrapped tightly around his neck. Holding her close, Trent grabbed a few towels before he left the room.

"Hey, sweetheart, it's ok," he cooed.

"I thought..." Katelyn started to say but stopped as she noticed Mike on the sofa. "Oh my God, what happened?"

Trent couldn't help but smile as she slid down his body and grabbed the towels from him. He mourned the loss of her pressed against him.

"Mike here was about to tell me, but he's got a silver bullet lodged inside him, so we need to get it out," Trent explained, and knelt next to her as she pressed the towel to the wound in an attempt to stop the blood flow.

"This is all my fault, isn't it?" she asked. Trent knew she would blame herself.

"It's all good, honey," Mike drawled out. "Anything for a lady in distress." He smirked and then groaned in pain.

"Katelyn, I'm sorry to ask this, but I need your help getting the bullet out. You have smaller hands than me." Trent hated to see her worried, her frown making him want to bring her into his arms and never let her go.

"Yes, of course. Just tell me what you want me to do."

Trent loved this woman. She had a resilience few ever showed. She was brave, and she was his.

Trent smiled as he showed her what he needed her to do. Yeah, she was his.

CHAPTER FOURTEEN

K atelyn looked at herself in the bathroom mirror and almost didn't recognise the girl smiling back at her. Gone was the fear that had been a permanent fixture in her eyes. Instead, they looked alive. Yes, she was currently covered in blood, and yes, she had just helped remove a silver bullet from a werewolf—something she could honestly say was never on her bucket list, especially when she was the reason for the wolf being injured—but when saw the look of pride in Trent's eyes as she did what he'd asked, she had felt her own pride swell. A sign of proof to herself that she wasn't the same scared bird she had been when she moved to London.

Her ex may try to scare her, but she now had

something she didn't have before. She had Trent. Katelyn grinned into the glass as she washed the blood from her hands, and her bird chirped and purred in her mind. Trent made her feel safe and protected. He showed her in deed and word that she was important and not just a commodity or a vessel for profit.

Katelyn still hadn't revealed what she was. She wanted to, but a small part of her was holding back. To tell Trent who and what she was would put her life and soul in his hands.

"But I already have," she answered herself, and she was right. She had already put those in his hands by simply being here. Her bird had chosen him first, and Katelyn's heart had quickly followed.

Everything about him was the opposite of Duncan, a man who she had thought she loved. Yet what she felt for Trent was so much more. Somehow, deep down inside, she knew that when she told Trent what she was, she wouldn't need to be afraid anymore. He would understand and protect her.

Bending her head, Katelyn washed her face. It was amazing how digging out a bullet could get blood everywhere. When she lifted her head, her eyes met those of Trent's, and her heart reacted, pounding against her chest.

"You all right?" he asked, and all she could do was nod. The feelings he brought out of her had been scary, but now she enjoyed them. Butterflies, coupled with that feeling you get on a rollercoaster, settled deep down within her. It was like a crush, but ten times more powerful.

"You did good out there, sweetheart." His praise made her blush, so she took some time to dry her face and try to create some semblance of calm. "Hey," he whispered, and she felt him wrap his arms around her waist and rest his head on the top of her own. Releasing the towel, she faced his reflection again and smiled.

"I'm ok. A little shell shocked, I think, but yeah, I'm ok," she admitted and felt him squeeze her gently.

"You did amazing, sweetheart. Thanks to you, the mutt is now snoring soundly on the sofa."

Katelyn couldn't help the giggle that forced its way out

"I like it when you smile," Trent admitted, and Katelyn blushed again. She felt like a silly little girl, but she loved the way he made her heart gallop. Shivers flowed up and down her spine as he bent to kiss her neck, the feeling of his lips on her skin like no other.

"I like the way you taste," he admitted, and Katelyn tipped her head to the side, giving him better access.

She couldn't answer him. The ability to talk had gone the moment he touched her.

"I like the way your body responds to mine," he murmured, and his eyes once again met hers in the mirror. Grey met amber and locked. Time itself could have frozen for all Katelyn cared. This moment in Trent's arms was perfect.

"I like it too," she admitted quietly but never looked away from his gaze.

"Good," he growled out and bent his head once again, sucking hard on the skin where her shoulder and neck met. Katelyn couldn't hold back the groan of pleasure as she let herself lean back into Trent's hold.

"I want you, Katelyn. I hurt from wanting you," he whispered against her skin, each word tightening the coil of need deep within her. Words that repeated in her mind. She wanted him too.

Katelyn let Trent turn her within the cage of his arms until grey met amber. The fire within the depths of his eyes pulled a gasp from Katelyn, not from fear, but from the fact she saw her own need reflected back at her.

"Trent," she whispered back, unable to form any more words. Her hands smoothed across his chest, each ridge of muscle defined under the black t-shirt he had put on. She missed the feel of his skin under her palms.

"Kiss me," she whispered again, her voice incapable of getting any louder, and when his lips touched her own, she sighed in pleasure. This felt right. This felt like home.

Katelyn was feeling brave, so, sliding her hands down, she reached the hem of Trent's T-shirt and lifted it, revealing rope after rope of tanned, perfect muscle. Stepping back slightly, Trent bent forward, helping her remove the offensive garment. When she dropped it to the floor, Katelyn looked her fill. She drank in the hard planes of his chest, lovingly gazed at each slab of muscle that defined his abdominal muscles, and followed the ridges that led under his jeans. Trent was, to her, a work of beautiful art.

"You keep looking at me like that, sweetheart, and I won't be responsible for my actions." Trent's deep voice pulled her gaze to his, but not before she saw his pecs shift and bounce, the muscles bunching as he moved. It was a move she had always found fascinating and sexy.

"I don't know what you mean," Katelyn answered innocently, leaning back against the sink. She had never been playful before, yet here, with Trent, she felt like she could be her true self.

"Oh, sweetheart, I think you do." He stalked closer, until only their breaths separated them. "If you don't watch it, I'm going to strip those jeans down those sexy legs of yours," he began, and Katelyn's breathing sped up. "Then I'm going to turn you around and bend you over this countertop."

His lips found her cheek.

"Slide those panties down." His lips reached her ear, tugging on the lobe, which nearly bucked her knees. "And let me bury my face in your pussy."

Katelyn gasped, then groaned, his words producing a mental picture that would have her climaxing before he touched her.

"I will eat you, Katelyn, until you scream my name and I taste you coming on my tongue." His voice had become a growl as he nibbled down her neck.

Katelyn's core clenched at his words. She was panting now, her body ready for whatever Trent had in mind. Only, he didn't follow through. Instead, he stood back up and smirked, before turning away and walking into the bedroom.

Trent's body was on fire, and it was his own fault. The words he had spoken to Katelyn to fuel her need for him had fuelled his own, until he felt like he was going to explode.

Seeing Katelyn tend to Mike, no questions asked, no complaining of the blood, had shown him how kind and brave she was. He knew she was scared about what was stalking her, but she trusted him to protect her. That alone would have brought him to his knees, but to see her looking at him with fire in her eyes had pushed him to his limits.

He didn't deny he wanted to do exactly what he had described he would do, but he wanted their first time to be special and not just a quickie against the sink. She was worth so much more than that.

Katelyn was a woman like no other, and when he made love to her, he wanted to erase any male who had come before him. Erase any memories and replace them with only him. Katelyn had brought out the caveman in him. Yes, he had always been protective—that was simply his nature —but with her, he wanted to carry her off and hide her from the world and any other men. The thought of her ex touching her had him ready to change and tear something apart.

Walking out of the bathroom was the hardest thing he had ever done. He wanted her—he hadn't lied when he said he hurt from wanting her. His cock was harder than when he was in his stone form, and the throbbing had only increased as he teased her.

A small growl erupted from Katelyn before he heard her move. He managed to turn in time to catch her as she vaulted into his arms, pushing him back onto the bed. Her lips sought his own, her tongue seeking immediate entrance.

Maybe Trent had pushed her a little far with his teasing. He grinned into the kiss as he palmed her ass cheeks and ground himself against her, pleased when she released his lips to moan out loud.

"You want this, sweetheart?" he asked as he pushed his cock against her jean clad pussy. Her scent of arousal filled the room.

"Oh God," she replied, and he chuckled and repeated the action.

"Not God, Trent... Remember that, 'cause you're going to be screaming it over and over again." His lips found hers once again, and this time, he took control, turning them on the bed so he could nestle into the cradle of her legs.

Katelyn's hands were frantic against his skin, touching everywhere she could. Taking both hands within one of his own, he pushed them above her head, pinning them to the mattress as he took total control.

Trent wanted to take his time, but his own need swirled, battling for dominance, driving him to push forward and claim his woman. Gritting his teeth, he held back, instead taking his free hand and letting the change affect only his forefinger. He gently pressed his long claw against the fabric of Katelyn's t-shirt and parted the material in one long rip, revealing her creamy breasts encased in dark blue satin. That sight alone would have sent him to his knees.

"Trent," her breathless voice called as she arched her back, pushing her breasts closer. Trent's heartrate was off the charts as he battled to take it slow. Pressing her hands into the mattress, he released them.

"Keep your hands there, sweetheart. Understood?" He waited until she nodded, her amber eyes on fire as she looked at him. Her lower lip caught in her teeth as he slowly moved lower.

Trent pressed gentle kisses to her stomach before laving her navel with his tongue. He looked up to check Katelyn had kept her hands where he had told her, and at the same time, he slowly released the button on her jeans. Going slow was killing him, but he would do it for her.

Kneeling back on the bed, Trent used his strength to lift her ass up while tugging her jeans down, taking her panties with them. Trent bit his lip. They matched the bra, and the dark blue against her pale, creamy skin made his cock pulse. He had never been this on edge before, never wanted to fire his load into his jeans from just looking at a woman before. But Katelyn was different, beautiful, and special.

"You're overdressed," Katelyn purred, her arms still above her head. She looked perfect, laid out and waiting.

"You're right." He smirked and slid from the bed. Unsnapping the buckle on his jeans, he dropped them to the floor, loving the sound Katelyn made as she drew in a breath. Trent could proudly boast he wasn't small. He was proportionate for his size, possibly bigger. Fisting himself, he watched Katelyn's eyes widen as her hips gyrated on the bed.

"You like what you see, sweetheart?"

"Uh huh," she answered and licked her lips.

"Fuck... Baby, you're testing my control," he admitted as he placed a knee back onto the mattress. Trent slowly slid his palms across her feet and ankles, before he grabbed her calves and pulled her down the bed. Her squeal of delight made him grin. Bending forward, he made quick work of her bra, leaving her naked to his gaze, and Trent drank her in.

He didn't think he would ever get tired of looking at her or touching her, and as he slid his hands up her thighs, he swore he would worship her for the rest of his life. Wrapping her legs around his waist, Trent brought Katelyn close; chest to chest, hip to hip, thigh to thigh. Her heat bathed his length as he rubbed it against her pussy.

"You ready for me?" he growled out and was rewarded by Katelyn squeezing her thighs and wrapping her arms around his neck. Her breath against his lips, he waited for her answer.

"I'm yours, Trent," she whispered, before she merged her lips with his own.

Trent reached down between them and fisted himself again, sweeping the tip against her swollen clit before gently starting to push. Inch by inch, her tight pussy swallowed his cock until, finally, he was in to the hilt.

This was what heaven was like. Surrounded by her heat, Trent was losing his battle to stay in control.

"Hold on tight," he gritted out as he palmed the back of her head, melded their lips together, and let loose, releasing all the pent-up need and lust he had felt since they first met.

Finally, Trent had found his home.

CHAPTER FIFTEEN

Duncan eyed the building in front of him. It had a large, glass front door and a small sign that read, **PSS – London Branch**.

He huffed a laugh. So, this was where their little visitor had run off to.

The werewolf had surprised them, but he hadn't gotten away unscathed. His team may be stupid, but they weren't completely useless. They had managed to shoot the slippery shit with a silver tracking bullet, something they had been using on paranormals for years. It was how Duncan had managed to capture so many for the black market.

Only now it would lead him to his greatest treasure. The werewolf was obviously in league with Katelyn, otherwise, why else would he have been snooping around the building where her flat was. Whatever the wolf knew, he would tell them, and then Duncan would do what he did best. He'd rip him limb from limb and sell the parts for profit. Werewolves were, after all, a wanted commodity—medicinal purposes and all that.

Duncan grinned and climbed back into the limo waiting for him. He was one step closer to catching Katelyn, a step closer to a payday that would see him settled and off the radar for those above him. It was either her or him, and if Duncan was frank, he would rather it be her.

She had been easy to seduce, to fool into thinking he had feelings for her when he was only after what her phoenix could provide. She was worth more to him as a vessel than an actual person.

"Are we close?" William asked from his slouched position in the back of the limo, a glass of whiskey in his hand.

"Yes, we're close. As soon as night falls, we will find the wolf and have some fun," Duncan stated with a sadistic smile. And fun they would have. It had been a while since Duncan had enjoyed some good old-fashioned torture. He missed the days when he could play with his prey, create a blood bath and let his true self free.

"We've almost run out of time," William admitted, and Duncan nodded as the limo pulled away, his own glass now filled.

"They will be here tomorrow, and by that time, we will have not only a phoenix, but a werewolf as well. All will be well."

"I hope you're right, Duncan. I hope you are right," William admitted.

"Me too," Duncan answered quietly, his thoughts turning to torture as the limo moved away from the building that housed the PSS. In only a few hours, they would be back, and then the fun will really start.

CHAPTER SIXTEEN

Trent pulled Katelyn harder against him, her body fitting like she had been made just for him. Her soft to his hard, her light to his dark. After what they had shared together, Trent couldn't imagine his life without her in it. The contentment he felt deep within him, where both sides of himself resided, was astounding—a shock to the system when usually they were fighting for dominance. Now their focus was on the curvy redhead nestled in his arms. The hours they had spent in his bed, he could honestly say, had been the best of his life.

Katelyn completed his soul. His mother had always said if he found a woman that could control his darker side, he would know she was the one.

Trent could say with conviction that if Katelyn said jump, the gargoyle within and his demon side would both chorus with how high.

Trent stroked his fingers up and down her bare arm as she slept, nuzzling against her neck. He knew she was exhausted, but he would never tire from touching her.

"Mmmm, you can't be horny again," she mumbled, and Trent nipped at her skin as he ground his semi hard cock against her ass.

"Always for you, sweetheart," he growled. This woman had turned him into a walking erection. He just had to think about touching her and he was hard.

"Well, you had best feed me if you want me to give in to your devilish ways, or I may waste away," Katelyn said with a smile as she turned in his arms. Her head rested on his bicep as she looked up into his eyes, her fingers stroking his chest, drawing small circles and making his heart pound.

"Keep that up and I will have you flat on your back again, sweetheart," he purred, before kissing the tip of her nose.

"Promises, promises," she answered. "But I want food first." Her giggle was music to his ears.

Trent smiled down at her, lost to the deep

amber of her eyes. "Then I had best feed the wench." He smirked and rolled out of bed, letting her head fall to the mattress.

"Wench? Who are you calling a wench?" Katelyn argued, and Trent couldn't resist leaning back over and kissing her hard.

"You are." He grinned as he slid a pair of jogging bottoms on. "Taking advantage of me like that."

"What?" she squealed, and as Trent left the room, a pillow followed. It felt good to laugh, felt good to relax and finally feel like he belonged. His bare feet made little sound as he moved into the open-plan living area. He would feed his woman and then spend another few hours in bed making her scream.

"I was wondering when you were going to venture out. I don't know how much more screaming of your name I could have handled," Mike called out from the sofa, his prone body still recovering after his near fatal injury.

"I guess I should apologise, but I'm not sorry," Trent replied and grinned. "Hungry?"

"Sodding famished. I am a wolf, you know. We require lots of sustenance," Mike responded.

"You know where the kitchen is. You could have helped yourself."

"But I'm dying," Mike complained, causing Trent to laugh.

"Well, isn't this cute," a new voice called out. Trent spun around to see four males walking into the room, one dressed in a suit and the others kitted out in military gear.

"Who the fuck are you?" Trent growled, claws instantly erupting from his fingertips. Instead of an answer, the lead male put his finger to his lips. Seconds later, Trent looked down to see a dart sticking out from his chest.

Voices around him became muffled. His vision tapered as whatever was in the dark took over.

Katelyn's screams were the last thing he heard as he fell into oblivion.

CHAPTER SEVENTEEN

Katelyn grinned and gave a little girly jiggle under the covers. For some reason, Trent brought out the cheeky side in her and made her want to be playful. Her body was sore as she stretched her arms over her head, but sore in such a good way. Trent had left no area untouched or absent of his kisses. He'd commanded her body like no other. His touch had been all it took to set her alight, but when they made love, he set her soul on fire. Her bird had wanted to break free, claim him, and soar to the heavens.

Grinning, Katelyn climbed out of bed. Yes, Trent had only just left the room, but she missed him already. She pulled one of his dark t-shirts out of the draw and slipped it on, along with her panties, and padded out of the room. Her thoughts on Trent, she was oblivious to the danger until she watched her male hit the floor.

"Trent...? *No!*" she screamed out as the man she loved dropped to the ground, his eyes rolling to the back of his head. His claws had erupted, but the men who did this to him had caught him so off guard he hadn't had a chance to fully change.

She had caused this.

Katelyn's hand flew to her mouth as she fought back a sob.

"Ahh, Katelyn," a husky voice said, gaining her attention. It was a voice that once had brought her shivers of delight, that once she had longed to hear. Now, it only caused dread and fear.

Duncan had found her.

Fear caused her body to tremble. Eyes wide, she turned to meet the man who had ruined her life and hunted her down. There was no running away for her; she realised that now. Even death couldn't bring her any peace, for her corpse could bring a profit.

"Duncan," she whispered.

"My dear. Oh, how I have missed you. I'm surprised to have found you so easily. I had just thought to catch the wolf and torture him for information, but..." Duncan sighed, "it looks like I've lost out on the fun again. Pity."

Katelyn didn't move as he stepped closer. The look he gave her as his gaze swept up and down her body made her stomach lurch. She wished she had put something else on besides Trent's shirt.

"I see you are looking lovely as ever." Katelyn hunched her shoulders as Duncan lifted a hand to touch her cheek. She hated his touch, had done since the day he hit her and made his true intentions known. How she had fallen for his little charade just showed how pathetic she had really been, how gullible she was.

But no more. She may have run away a frightened little bird, but she wasn't anymore.

She had experienced more life in a day with Trent than she had in her whole existence. Trent had shown her what true feelings, true passion, was like. Katelyn would not go down without a fight. Even if it killed her.

"I hate you," Katelyn spat out, and jerked her face away from his touch.

"Oh, I know." Duncan smirked and then gripped her chin, his fingers digging into her skin, no doubt leaving bruises.

"You will regret running away, little birdy." He released her and pushed her back into the waiting arms of the man who had found her in the park. Her gaze landed on Trent again before she flicked it over to where Mike had been. He had been dragged from the sofa, his curses earning him a punch to the jaw.

"William, let's adjourn to the roof to wait for our ride home. Meanwhile, the boys here will deal with..." He gestured to Trent sprawled on the floor and a pinned Mike. "Make sure there is nothing left," Duncan drawled on, before he turned and moved past Katelyn.

Mike was pinned to the floor, his injuries still too severe to fight. Katelyn's eyes met those of the wolf's, and sadness was reflected back at her. Katelyn could do little as she was dragged away, but mouthed, *I'm sorry*, to Mike.

Her gaze, though, flew to Trent. She didn't know if he was breathing or if he was already dead. A sob fought its way up her throat as she fought against William's hold.

"Trent," she whispered, and was rewarded with a slap to the face and a hard tug on her hair.

"Shut up, bitch." William's red eyes came into

view. Anger and hatred blazed in their depths. "You have caused us enough trouble."

"Fuck you," Katelyn spat out, using what little bravery she had left.

Katelyn welcomed the awaiting cold darkness as she saw a large fist approaching her face. There would be only a moment of pain and then blissful silence, and she welcomed it. It was better than dealing with a broken heart.

Mike watched as Katelyn was dragged away. The punch to her face had made him wince, but it had also stirred his anger. Violence against women was something he hated with a passion. It was in his wolf nature to care for them and protect them. Only, in this instance, he had failed. He had seen the fear in her eyes—it was almost tangible—yet he was helpless to do anything about it.

The bullet wound he had sustained was more serious than he initially thought. Puncturing his liver, he was lucky to be alive. It was taking his healing abilities a little longer to repair the damage.

His hope that Trent was alive was vanishing with each second. There wasn't much that could knock out a gargoyle, especially one of Trent's size. Along with him being a crossbreed, there was really only one sure fire way of keeping him down, and that was killing him.

The whole situation looked about as fucked up as it could get. Mike couldn't fight, Trent was out, and there were two goons looking at him like their Christmas had just come early.

Great.

His mother had always said he wouldn't be able to talk his way out of every situation, and she had been right. Though even if he somehow got out of this breathing, he would never tell her that.

"Oh, boys," a husky voice said from the hall-way. The seductive tone had the two males turning in an instant and releasing Mike's scruff. Eyes wide, Mike watched as his boss, the main woman in charge of the PSS, sauntered in.

What shocked Mike the most was what Suzanna was wearing. Gone was the office attire and taking its place were leather trousers that was so snug they could have been painted on, and a matching halter top. Her hair was, as usual, braided down her back. She looked lethal, even without taking into account the weapon she held in her hand: a broadsword that even most males of

Mike's size would struggle to lift. Yet she did—with style.

The sword spun in an arch as she displayed her skill. All the while, a lethal gleam shone in her eyes.

"Michael, darling, be a peach and see if you can wake our American boy up, would you," she purred and winked over at him before stepping up against the two burly bodyguards. Mike was mesmerised by her skill.

"Mike, now!" she shouted, reminding him of what he needed to do. Gripping his side, he got to his feet slowly and limped towards Trent. Falling to his knees, he tried to roll the big guy over, but his size was against him.

"Jesus Christ on a crutch, Trent. What the fuck have you been eating, dinosaur steaks? Fuck me." Sweat poured down Mike's face as he finally managed to get Trent onto his side.

"Come on, big man, wake up." Mike felt for a pulse and let out a breath of relief as he found it strong and steady. Mike could still hear the sounds of battle behind him—well, more like Suzanna kicking some serious arse if the cursing was anything to go by. And here he thought his boss was a lady.

Mike snorted. Frowning, he forced one of Trent's eyelids open, only to find his pupil dilated and unresponsive. Sitting back, he pulled his fist back and fired a shot at Trent's face.

Nothing—except pain on Mike's part. Trent's face was hard as rock.

"Anything?" Suzanna asked as she knelt next to Mike. The scent of blood hung from her.

"Nothing—well, I think I've broken my hand." He held it up to show her.

"Stop being a baby. Right, I think I may know a way to wake him, but it's a risk," Suzanna admitted as she got up and hunted through the draws of the kitchen.

"I'm not a baby." Mike pouted and got up quickly as Suzanna bent down and lit Trent's joggers on fire.

"What the fuck are you doing, woman? Are you out of your bloody mind?" Mike moved to pat Trent's leg down but was stopped by the harsh grip of Suzanna. His eyes locked with hers, whose silver swirled, almost like mercury.

"Don't! You will see," she answered, but didn't elaborate. With her help, Mike moved with her until they were hiding behind the sofa. The smell of burning filled the flat.

"What have you done?" Mike asked again, confusion filling his head and making him wonder if he wasn't already knocked out and dreaming.

"You will see," was all Suzanna said, moments before an inhuman roar filled the room.

CHAPTER EIGHTEEN

Darkness gave away to fire; consuming fire that didn't hurt. Swirls of reds, oranges and golds filled his mind. Strength filled Trent as consciousness slowly returned, along with a new sense of power.

Eyes wide, if only for a second, his body was consumed by flame. It caressed his skin like a lover and gave him a sense of completion he had been missing his whole life. Power and strength ripped through him, causing his muscle mass to grow and pulling a roar from him.

Now he knew what he was, what his mother had been so frightened about.

He was a fire demon.

Memories flooded his system; memories of his

friends, his life, and one small female who had become the centre of his world.

"Katelyn," he breathed. Memories of the attack filled his head, along with shame that he had been unable to protect her. He roared again, roared his pain and anguish.

"Trent," a voice called out. He turned his bulk towards the sound and found a female and male looking at him, hands up to show they meant him no harm.

"Trent," the female called again, and Trent, this time, noticed she was covered in blood. His nostrils flared as he caught the metallic stench, and then he found two bodies practically cut in half. Trent stepped forward.

"Trent, you need to listen," she said, and he remembered her as Suzanna. Friend.

"They have Katelyn," she told him, and he snarled. Suzanna winced but held her ground. "On the roof," was all she said, and all Trent heard, before he moved, his speed surprising considering his bulk. Trent's only thoughts were of Katelyn; his woman... his mate.

The fire had died down and no longer caressed his skin, but it had also taken his clothing. Naked, he flew up the stairs, not caring who saw him, before he erupted through the door that led to the roof. Two men turned to look at him, shock etched upon their faces as he stalked closer.

Trent inhaled, catching a myriad of scents. These men were demons, and they had his female. Her unconscious form could be seen laid out on the floor of the helicopter behind them.

"Well, isn't he a big boy," one of the males joked, and Trent snarled, showing off his new fangs. He felt a change overcome his body once again, this time a familiar one. His gargoyle skin flowed over his form, hardening flesh and turning it to stone.

Fire and stone, that's what he was, and nothing would stop him. His steps were loud as he stalked his prey.

"William, you deal with our new friend," the other male said quickly and climbed into the helicopter. "Take off. Now!" he screamed as Trent reached the first male—William. The male was nothing to him. Taking his neck with his large hand, he lifted the male from the ground. Trent's eyes found the still form of his mate, and he snarled.

The scent of fear filled his nose, making him want to sneeze. Instead, he brought the male closer.

"You hurt her." It wasn't a question. Trent already knew that both these males had hurt his mate. It was a statement. One that would have swift retribution.

"You die!" he snarled and squeezed. In seconds, the male's neck broke, the snap satisfying but not nearly satisfying enough.

As Trent dropped the male, the helicopter lifted off the ground. The male within, the one Trent now identified as the male that had been stalking Katelyn, grinned and waved.

"Buh-bye now," he called out, only to gasp in horror as Trent reached up and grabbed the helicopter's landing skids. Using his newfound strength, Trent pulled. The helicopter groaned in response, the rotors whirring faster. Trent wasn't worried about them. He was made of stone, nothing could penetrate his skin.

With a roar, Trent tugged the helicopter down hard onto the concrete roof, blowing the engine and grounding the bird. Cries of pain could be heard from the pilots, but Trent ignored them, instead snarling as he ripped away wreckage to find his prey.

Bright red eyes met his as the other male erupted from the carriage, his grotesque features a total opposite of the mortal form he used to hide his true self. Wings kept him above ground as he snarled at Trent.

"You idiot. You have no idea who you are dealing with, and once I kill you, the phoenix will still be mine." The words were followed by a snarl as the demon dived at Trent, clawed hands outstretched, aiming for his neck. Trent had little time to take in what he had said.

Trent stretched his neck side to side, enjoying the crack, before he turned at the last minute, letting the demon sweep past him, but only just. Grabbing the demon's wings, Trent pulled and laughed as they ripped free, extracting a scream of agony from the male. Blood erupted from the wounds, yet that didn't stop Trent.

Trent stalked the male as he writhed on the ground, his body spasming from the pain. "You hurt her," he growled out as he stood over the male. "You hurt my mate."

"Fuck you," the demon spat out.

"You die," Trent snarled in response and planted a foot in the centre of the male's chest. The heavy stone weighed down on the male as he started to beg.

"Please don't kill me. I'm sorry. I'm sorry I hurt

her. Please!" he implored, yet Trent ignored his pleas. Trent wanted justice.

"You die," Trent repeated and stepped down. In one motion, the demon's chest crushed inwards, killing him in a spray of blood. Satisfaction coursed through Trent and he let out a roar of victory. His body throbbed with power, and he longed to give in to it. Let it overtake his body and destroy everything.

"Trent! Quick, the helicopter... it's about to explode," Suzanna called out, causing Trent to spin around.

"Katelyn!" he shouted and sprinted for the broken carriage. *"Katelyn,"* he called again, panic overtaking his voice. Just as he reached the broken door, the helicopter exploded, catapulting Trent across the roof and against the wall.

Pain tore through him as he watched it burn, watched his mate burn, and Trent roared out his anguish.

Katelyn woke slowly and was greeted by flame.

Flame to her made everything better. It was her friend, and she embraced it. She heard the explosion yet felt no pain. She heard a roar but couldn't place it.

Memories of what had happened filtered through her mind. Fear, followed by anger, followed by grief. Grief for the male she loved, for the male her and her bird had chosen as their mate. Grief for a life they wouldn't have.

Katelyn emptied her grief, collected it and poured it into a basin in the back of her mind. She let it run until nothing was left and only flame remained.

Arching her back, she embraced the fire, letting it consume her until only ashes were left. This was what she was.

She was a phoenix, and she would be born from the ashes.

CHAPTER NINETEEN

Trent could do little but watch the flames as they burned brighter and higher into the dark night. He was too shocked for tears, yet inside he was crying. Grief hit him hard, crippling him like nothing he had ever experienced before.

One day. He had only had one day with the woman he loved. *One day*. It wasn't enough. Eternity wouldn't be enough. Yet he had only had one day.

"Not enough," Trent whispered.

"Trent," Suzanna's voice filtered through the haze of pain and sorrow.

"Trent," she called again, and this time, he lifted his gaze to hers. He expected sympathy. Instead, he got a glare.

"Get off your large stony arse and get into that fire. Now!"

"What?" Confused, he frowned up at her before looking at the blaze.

"Ugh, men. Sometimes you guys can be so damn stupid." She paused and tilted her head as she looked at him and smiled. "Ok, let's explain this in Mike terms, shall we. You." She pointed at his chest. "You, my dear, are a gargoyle."

"Yes, I know."

Suzanna shushed him. "I wasn't finished, rocks for brains." She raised an eyebrow, and Trent nodded for her to continue. Her glare had gone, instead it was replaced with a smile of affection.

"You are gargoyle, and...?" She paused again. Trent had always known he was a crossbreed; he just didn't know much about his other side. Suzanna scoffed when he didn't answer her question. "You are also a fire demon."

Suzanna watched him and waited, but when no reply came to him, she sighed.

"Oh, for fuck's sake. You don't burn, dickhead. You didn't burn downstairs when I set your pants on fire and your flames came to the surface, and you won't now. So *get up*." Suzanna pushed him until he relented and stood.

"There's no point." He sighed, his eyes still on the flames. "I may not burn, but..." He couldn't finish the sentence.

"Oh, my giddy aunt, are you kidding me? Did she not tell you what she was?" Suzanna placed her hands on her hips and glared again at Trent. "Did you not hear what the demon said about Katelyn before you stomped on his chest?"

"He said he had hurt her," Trent answered.

"Before that."

"He was going to kill me."

"After that! And think hard, Trent, because if you get this wrong, I may have to rethink us working together, because no one can be this dense," Suzanna growled out and walked over to an air-conditioning vent. She perched on it and waited, her arms folded across her chest.

Trent thought back to his small battle with the male that had taken Katelyn, remembered seeing her unconscious form in the helicopter. The male's words repeated in his head, over and over

You idiot. You have no idea who you are dealing with, and once I kill you, the phoenix will still be mine

The phoenix...

He frowned.

Katelyn was a phoenix. Everything came together in his head; why she was on the run, why the demons were desperate for her, and...

Trent bolted for the ball of fire that was the remnant of the helicopter.

"*Ding, ding, ding,* we have a winner," Suzanna said as he ran. The fire was ignored as he reached the wreckage. His world narrowed to one purpose as he pulled broken metal out of the way until he knelt down within the ash.

There, peeking up at him, was a set of amber eyes. A phoenix risen from the ashes. This time, Trent allowed the tears to flow as he scooped up the small bird in his arms and walked out of the fire.

Suzanna watched them leave the roof and sighed. One mission down, Odin knows how many more to go. Her task when she had been sent to earth was simple: protect the paranormals. But it wasn't just about protecting. It was about showing them that life wasn't just about surviving. They could be happy; they could thrive.

She had been lucky this time, picking up on

her charges distress. Meaning, she had time to react and assist as needed.

Lifting her hands, Suzanna closed her eyes and channelled the power the gods had given her. Lightning struck all around her, erasing the evidence of battle and the two demons Trent had executed. Pride coursed through her when she thought of the male. He was strong and would be a great assistance.

Sighing again, she turned, her work done for now. She stopped when she saw the deep blue eyes of a werewolf. "Mike, you should be resting," she said flippantly.

"I know what you are," he whispered in awe.

With a flip of her hair, Suzanna smirked, then blew him a kiss before she left the roof, leaving a stunned wolf behind. Something about that male made her smile, even if he was a smartarse. Regardless, he had better keep his mouth shut or she would shut it for him. But using what method, she wasn't sure. Mouth or sword, the outcome would be the same.

Silence.

CHAPTER TWENTY

Katelyn stretched and felt nothing but softness beneath her. Her body was warm, and she felt more rested than she ever had in her life. Nothing ached. She grinned as she arched her back but felt something hard behind her. Slowly, she turned her head and met the dark eyes of Trent.

"Trent," she whispered, afraid to believe she was seeing him. "Oh my God, is it really you?" She turned quickly and cupped his face within her hands. "I saw you fall. You wouldn't wake up." Katelyn let the tears fall.

"Shhhh, it's ok," his deep voice answered as he covered her hands with his own. Bringing her palm

163

forward, he kissed it. "As you can see, sweetheart, I'm far from dead. In fact..."

Katelyn gasped as Trent grabbed her around the waist and pulled her on top of him, making sure she could feel his large erection.

"I'm about as far from dead as you can get, and very much happy to see you awake." He grinned up at her, and Katelyn couldn't help but grin back.

"What happened? Duncan... he was here." Katelyn couldn't help the shiver of fear that skated down her spine.

"Shh, baby, it's fine." Trent pulled her closer, until she could rest her head on his large chest. His hands caressed up and down her spine, chasing the shiver away.

"Duncan won't be able to hurt you ever again," Trent's deep voice confirmed, and Katelyn felt a weight lift from her shoulders. One she had carried for a long time.

"You killed him?" she asked. Strange, but she needed to know the details, needed to know he had no chance of coming back.

"Yes, I did. A foot through the chest will certainly do it," Trent admitted as he cupped her cheek again and lifted her gaze to his own. "I nearly lost you, and for that, I am sorry Katelyn.

You trusted me to protect you and I nearly failed."
His anguish hurt her own heart.

"But you didn't fail. I'm here with you
now. You destroyed them. You saved me,"
Katelyn cooed and pressed her lips to his palm.
This male had done what he promised and
more. He had become the centre of her
universe.

"Trent, I love you," she whispered as she
looked into his grey eyes.

"That's good," he answered, "because I love
you, my little firebird." Katelyn blushed but smiled.
He now knew everything about her. He knew what
she was yet loved her all the same.

Running away had been what she thought was
the bravest thing she ever did, when in fact it was
loving Trent and letting him see her for what she
truly was. This was her bravest deed.

Lifting up, Katelyn pressed her lips to his,
before pulling away yet staying close enough for
them to share breath.

"Trent, my bird chose you the minute we met.
Will you be my mate?" she asked, a part of her still
scared, only it didn't last long.

"Katelyn, you are a part of my soul. I will love
you for eternity and longer if the gods should allow.

You are already my mate in here." He took her hand and placed it over his heart.

Katelyn beamed up at the male who had stolen her heart and claimed her bird. Pressing her lips to his, she lost herself to her mate, lost herself to the love she had finally found, embracing it as only a phoenix could.

Whoever thought a gargoyle would catch a phoenix...

The End

ALSO BY J THOMPSON

SoulMate Series

SoulKiss Book 1

SoulFate Book 2

SoulDeath Book 3

SoulScarred Book 4 (coming 2019)

Dark Desire Series

Dark Confusion Book 1

Dark Need Book 2

Trinity Series

Ebony Book 1

Ivory Book 2 (coming 2019)

SoulReaper Series

Demon of my Dreams (TBC)

Cupid's Essence (Soulmate Series Spin off)

Exercise in Love (Stand alone)

Dragon Fire and Phoenix Ash- A collaboration between Mina Carter and J Thompson

COMING 2019

Blood Oath
A Dark Legacy Novel

Her glare made Marcus smirk. God, she was stunning when fired up. He stood and stalked towards her, watching as her eyes widened and her arms fell to the side while she backed up a step. Each step he took, she took one back, until her back was against the wall. Lifting his arms, Marcus placed his hands either side of her head, caging her in. Her scent filled his senses, making it harder to concentrate on anything but tasting her.

"What-what are you doing," she demanded nervously. He watched as she licked her lips, her gaze flicking from his mouth and back up to his eyes.

"Making you listen," he whispered, and bent his head to run his nose up her neck. Her vein pulsed, making his mouth water and his fangs ache. She was a tempting morsel that he doubted he would ever get enough of. As he moved up her neck to her ear, he growled.

"I wasn't six years old when I met your grandfather, Grace. I was thirty-four." She shivered under his touch, and he relished in the reaction.

"How..." she breathed out. "How old are you now?" Her voice was the barest of whispers.

"I'm thirty-four, Grace," he replied. It was a lie, technically. He had stopped ageing at thirty-four. His true age was more along the lines of three hundred plus.

Printed in Great Britain
by Amazon